A King Production presents…

Keep The Family Close…

A Novel

JOY DEJA KING

ISBN 13: 978-1942217374
ISBN 10: 1-942217-37-4
Cover concept by Joy Deja King
Cover Model: Joy Deja King

Library of Congress Cataloging-in-Publication Data;
King, Deja Joy
The Legacy: a novel/by Joy Deja King

For complete Library of Congress Copyright info visit;
www.joydejaking.com Twitter: @joydejaking

A King Production
P.O. Box 912, Collierville, TN 38027

A King Production and the above portrayal logo are trademarks of A King Production LLC

This Book is Dedicated To My:

Family, Readers, and Supporters.
I LOVE you guys so much. Please believe that!!

The Legacy...

A Trilogy

"If I Ever Loved You, I'll Always Love You,
That's How I Was Raised..."

Keep The Family Close...

Drake

A KING PRODUCTION

The Legacy

Keep The Family Close...

A Novel

JOY DEJA KING

Chapter One

Raised By Wolves

"Alejo, we've been doing business for many years and my intention is for there to be many more. But I do have some concerns…"

"That's why we're meeting today," Alejo interjected, cutting Allen off. I've made you a very wealthy man. You've made millions and millions of dollars from my family…"

"And you've made that and much more from our family," Clayton snapped, this time being the one to cut Alejo off. "So let's acknowledge this being a mutual beneficial relationship between both of our families."

Alejo slit his eyes at Clayton, feeling disrespected, his anger rested upon him. Clayton was the youngest son of Allen Collins but also the most vocal. Alejo then turned towards his son Damacio who sat calmly not saying a word in his father's defense, which further enraged the dictator of the Hernandez family. An ominous quietness engulfed the room as the Collins family remained seated on one side of the table and the Hernandez family occupied the other.

"I think we can agree that over the years we've created a successful business relationship that works for all parties involved," Kasir said, speaking up and trying to be the voice of reason and peacemaker for what was quickly turning into enemy territory. "No one wants to create new problems. We only want to fix the one we currently have so we can all move forward."

"Kasir, I've always liked you," Alejo said with a half smile. "You've continuously conducted yourself with class and respect. Others can learn a lot from you."

"Others, meaning your crooked ass nephews," Clayton barked not ignoring the jab Alejo was taking at him. He then pointed his finger at Felipe and Hector, making sure that everyone at the table knew exactly who he was speaking of since there were a dozen family members on the Hernandez side of the table.

Chaos quickly erupted within the Hernandez family as the members began having a heated exchange amongst each other. They were speaking Spanish and although neither Allen nor Clayton understood what was being said, Kasir spoke the language fluently.

"Dad, I think we need to fall back and not let this

meeting get any further out of control. Let's table this discussion for a later date," Kasir told his father in a very low tone.

"Fuck that! We ain't tabling shit. As much money as we bring to this fuckin' table and these snakes want to short us. Nah, I ain't having it. That shit ends today," Clayton stated, not backing down.

"You come here and insult me and my family with your outrageous accusations," Alejo stood up and yelled, pushing back the single silver curl that kept falling over his forehead. "I will not tolerate such insults from the likes of you. My family does good business. You clearly cannot say the same."

"This is what you call good business," Clayton shot back, placing his iPhone on the center of the table. Then pressing play on the video that was sent to him.

Alejo grabbed the phone from off the table and watched the video intently, scrutinizing every detail. After he was satisfied he then handed it to his son Damacio, who after viewing, passed it around to the other family members at the table.

"What's on that video?" Kasir questioned his brother.

"I want to know the same thing," his father stated.

"Let's just say that not only are those two motherfuckers stealing from us, they're stealing from they own fuckin' family too," Clayton huffed, leaning back in his chair, pleased that he had the proof to back up his claims.

"We owe your family an apology," Damacio said, as his father sat back down in his chair with a glaze of defeat in his eyes. It was obvious the old man hated to be wrong and had no intentions of admitting it, so his son had to do it for him.

"Does that mean my concerns will be addressed and handled properly?" Allen Collins questioned.

"Of course. You have my word that this matter will be corrected in the very near future and there is no need for you to worry, as it won't happen again. Please accept my apology on behalf of my entire family," Damacio said, reaching over to shake each of their hands.

"Thank you, Damacio," Allen said giving a firm handshake. "I'll be in touch soon."

"Of course. Business will resume as usual and we look forward to it," Damacio made clear before the men gathered their belongings and began to make their exit.

"Wait!" shouted Alejo. The Collins men stopped in their tracks and turned towards him.

"Father, what are you doing?" Damacio asked, confused by his sudden outburst.

"There is something that needs to be addressed and no one is leaving this room until it's done," Alejo demanded.

With smooth ease, Clayton rested his arm towards the back of his pants, placing his hand on the Glock 20–10mm auto. Before the meeting, the Collins' men had agreed to have their security team wait outside in the parking lot instead of coming in the building, so it wouldn't be a hostile environment. But that didn't stop Clayton from taking his own precautions. He eyed his brother Kasir who maintained his typical calm demeanor that annoyed the fuck out of Clayton.

"Alejo, what else needs to be said that wasn't already discussed?" Allen asked, showing no signs of distress.

"Please, come take a seat," Alejo said politely. Allen stared at Alejo then turned to his two sons and nodded his head as the three men walked back towards their chairs.

Alejo wasted no time and immediately began his over the top speech. "I was born in Mexico and raised by wolves. I was taught that you kill or be killed. When I rose to power by slaughtering my enemies and my friends, I felt no shame," Alejo stated, looking around at everyone sitting at the table. His son Damacio swallowed hard as his Adam's apple seemed to be throbbing out of his neck.

"As I got older and had my own family, I decided I didn't want that for my children. I wanted them to understand the importance of loyalty, honor, and respect," Alejo said proudly, speaking with his thick Spanish accent, which was heavier than usual. He moved away from his chair and began to pace the floor as he spoke. "Without understanding the meaning of being loyal, honoring, and respecting your family, you're worthless. Family forgives but some things are unforgivable so you have no place on this earth or in my family."

Then, without warning and before anyone had even noticed, blood was squirting from Felipe's slit throat. With the same precision and quickness, Alejo took his sharp pocketknife and slit Hector's throat too. Everyone was too stunned and taken aback to stutter a word.

Alejo wiped the blood off his pocketknife on the white shirt that a now dead Felipe was wearing. He kept wiping until the knife was clean. "That is what happens when you are disloyal. It will not be tolerated... ever." Alejo made direct contact with each of his family members at the round table before focusing on Allen. "I want to personally apologize to you and your sons. I do not condone what Felipe and Hector did and they have now paid the price with their lives."

"Apology accepted," Allen said.

"Yeah, now let's get the fuck outta here," Clayton whispered to his father as the three men stood in unison, not speaking another word until they were out the building.

"What type of shit was that?" Kasir mumbled.

"I told you that old man was fuckin' crazy," Clayton said shaking his head as they got into their waiting SUV.

"I think we all knew he was crazy just not that crazy. Alejo know he could've slit them boys' throats after we left," Allen huffed. "He just wanted us to see the fuckin' blood too and ruin our afternoon," he added before chuckling.

"I think it was more than just that," Clayton replied, looking out the tinted window as the driver pulled out the parking lot.

"Then what?" Kasir questioned.

"I think old man Alejo was trying to make a point, not only to his family members but to us too."

"You might be right, Clayton."

"I know I'm right. We need to keep all eyes on Alejo 'cause I don't trust him. He might've killed his crooked ass nephews to show good faith but trust me that man hates to ever be wrong about anything. What he did to his nephews is probably what he really wanted to do to us but he knew nobody would've left that building alive. The only truth Alejo spoke in there was he was raised by wolves," Clayton scoffed leaning back in the car seat.

All three men remained silent for the duration of the drive. Each pondering what had transpired in what was supposed to be a simple business meeting that turned into a double homicide. They also thought about the point Clayton said Alejo was trying to make. No one wanted that to be true as their business with the Hernandez family was a lucrative one for everyone involved. But for men like Alejo, sometimes pride held more value than the almighty dollar, which made him extremely dangerous.

Chapter Two

Beauty Fades...Love Is Always

Allen watched from a distance, as his wife Karmen, meticulously moisturized her long and toned legs. The tip of her toes was perched in the center of the marble bathroom floor on the luxury Italian mink beige bench. Her many years as a dancer gave her the legs that any woman would envy.

Allen stood for a second; feeling like it was only yesterday he saw her performing in a ballet in New York

City. She stood out like a rare diamond. Not just because she was the only woman of color but also because she was simply the best one on the stage. That night always brought a mischievous smile to Allen's face because he actually attended the show with his then girlfriend, who insisted they went although he had no interest. But after seeing the beautiful ballerina, Allen couldn't stay away. He popped up at every performance and began flooding her dressing room with flowers after each show. The woman Allen had become so enchanted with had no idea who her mystery admirer was, until a month later, when he was waiting for her after her nightly performance with an exquisite bouquet of flowers in his hand and an invitation to dinner.

When she saw the tall handsome man, who was perfectly groomed in his tailored suit, she couldn't resist his offer. After their dinner, Allen had decided that the dancer would one day become his wife. He literally swept Karmen off her feet and one year later, she traded in her dream of becoming a world-renowned ballerina to being Mrs. Allen Collins.

"How long have you been standing there?" Karmen questioned, clearly startled when she realized her husband had been staring at her.

"Not long enough," Allen smiled when Karmen began to pull down her silk slip. "Don't stop because of me. I was enjoying the show," he said, continuing to smile.

"You're so bad," Karmen giggled.

"And you love it," he countered, kissing his wife on the lips. For him, kissing Karmen still felt as magical as the first time.

"Always so sure of yourself. But you're right, I do love it. I love everything about you except for the fact you're always late," she said slapping him playfully on the shoulder. "You know we have to be at the gala in an hour, so hurry up!"

"I'm about to get in the shower right now and I'll be ready to go in thirty minutes. I know how important tonight is."

"Good. So stop flirting with me and go get in that shower before you talk me into doing something that we just don't have time for," Karmen teased.

"Oh. we can always make time for that," Allen flirted back as he started taking off his clothes.

"Bye, Allen! I'm off to get dressed," Karmen said disappearing out of the bathroom. She headed towards her elaborate closet that would make any label whore slit their wrist for.

Karmen slipped on the custom designed Zuhair Murad dress and did a complete 360 in the full-length mirror.

"Wow, this is even more beautiful than the sketches I approved," she commented in awe of the gown. With its sweetheart neckline and fishtail hem, it was the contrast of a sheer, ethereal white and edgy metallic belt that truly made it a stunner. The fabric glided down each curve of her body, giving the perfect silhouette.

"What did I do to deserve you?"

Karmen looked up from staring at herself in the mirror and noticed her husband standing in the hallway. "Maybe because you're the most incredible man I've ever met."

The two of them locked eyes for a few seconds with neither saying a word. They had been married for over twenty years and shared three beautiful kids together. They had more money than most could even dream of. With all the time that had passed, their love appeared to remain intact. Their life seemed perfect...almost too perfect.

"Omigosh, how long is this boring shindig supposed to last," Ashton sighed as she sipped her champagne.

"Can you keep your voice down," Kasir advised. "You're the daughter of the man being honored. It doesn't look good if anyone hears you complaining."

"Duh, I doubt anyone can even hear their own thoughts with this classical music blasting through the building. Where's the DJ?" Ashton said looking around the room.

Clayton's date, Vannette, couldn't hold back her laughter at Ashton's comment. But when he shot her a menacing glare, she immediately got in line and shut up. "Why did you even come, Ashton? I'm surprised you showed up," Clayton asked.

"Trust me, it wasn't by choice. Mother threatened to cut off my allowance for the month if I didn't come. I'm going to Miami on Saturday for two weeks to party with some of my girlfriends, so I need all my coins," Ashton hissed, flipping her long medium brown ombre colored hair to the side.

"Get out! The Miami trip is this Saturday? I thought it was next Saturday?" Clayton's date Vannette, who was also one of Ashton's best friends questioned.

"No bitch, it's this Saturday," Ashton snapped. "So, you better have your shit together 'cause it's gonna be a blast!"

"You didn't ask me if you could go to Miami," Clayton stated giving Vannette the stare of death.

"Umm, you guys have only been dating what like six weeks. She doesn't need your permission," Ashton grumbled.

"Mind your business," Clayton warned his sister.

"I'm not one of your play things. You can't tell me shit." Ashton rolled her eyes and sipped some more of her champagne.

"You've had enough to drink. I think you should put your glass down," Kasir suggested.

"I could've sworn that I turned twenty-one last month and since neither one of you look like my father, I suggest you tend to your own situations. I'm good over here." Ashton gave a devilish smirk to both Kasir and Clayton before turning away.

The brothers decided to ignore their younger sister because they both knew it was a battle they would lose. Between the three of them, it was a well-known fact that Ashton was the untouchable one in their father's eyes. She could do no wrong even when it was obvious she was dead wrong. The only person that could yield any sort of power over Ashton was their mother. She loved her daughter but wasn't under a spell like their father seemed to be when it came to his little princess.

"Daddy, where did you disappear to!" Ashton's eyes lit up and beamed when her father came back to the table. "You know I only came so I could spend time with you."

"I know, my love," he grinned, kissing his daughter on her cheek. "But there are a lot of people I do business with here, so it's part of my job to make sure I thank each of them personally for coming tonight," he explained.

"I totally understand," she said lovingly. "But I have an exam tomorrow and I really need to get home and study. Do you mind if I go ahead and leave?" her eyes looking up at her father so sweet and innocently.

"Of course not. I'm just glad you came."

"Thanks, daddy." Ashton stood up and gave her father a hug. "You're the best. Tell mom I said bye."

"I will. Let me walk you out," Allen said leaving the table with his daughter.

"I gotta hand it to Ashton, she somehow always manages to get her way and keep our father under her thumb at the same time," Kasir laughed.

"Glad you think it's funny. I think it's ridiculous. If we tried to leave before this gala was officially over, father would go nuclear. But because Ashton comes up with some bullshit story, it must be true. His little princess might have the face of an angel but she definitely plays with the devil." Clayton gritted his teeth.

"You would know," Vannette mumbled under her breath, wishing she could've left with her friend.

"What did you say?" Clayton asked checking to see if he heard Vannette correctly before giving her a tongue thrashing.

"I said she would never let her father know though," Vannette said recovering smoothly.

"Oh. Yeah, my lil' sis might think she's got our father fooled but one day the blinders will come off."

"Here comes mom, so let's chill on all this Ashton talk," Kasir said, acknowledging his mother when she got to the table. "Mom, did I tell you how absolutely beautiful you look tonight. You make me so proud."

"Kasir, it's not good to make your mother blush, but thank you."

"You really do look stunning, mother. I hope father appreciates what he has." Karmen gave her son a peculiar look but dismissed it since Clayton frequently made comments that came across as odd or inappropriate sometimes.

"Thank you, Clayton, and I'm sure your father appreciates what he has. Speaking of your father, where is he? He said he was coming back to the table."

"He did but Ashton had to leave and he wanted to walk her out." Kasir informed his mother.

"Ashton left?"

"Yes, she had to get home and study for an exam she has tomorrow," Clayton added sarcastically. Karmen shrugged her shoulders like she knew her daughter was full of shit but didn't have the time to entertain the lie.

"Let me go find your father. The gala is ending shortly and he needs to give his closing remarks before everyone starts leaving. I'll be back."

Karmen made her way through the crowd, smiling at some of the guests and stopping to personally talk to the ones that were important to Allen. This was her life; making sure things went smoothly especially when it came to business. Allen Collins might've been the head of a lucrative drug empire but to everyone attending the gala, he was a highly respected CEO of a multimillion dollar private equity firm. He had the perfect wife by his side to perpetuate his façade.

"Excuse me, I think I see my husband." Karmen smiled leaving the couple she was talking to and headed towards Allen. As she got a little closer, Karmen slowed down her stride. Allen was off to the side with another man and a woman. He seemed to be in the midst of a highly intense conversation but it wasn't with the man but with the woman. This uneasiness flooded her soul and Karmen tried her best to shake it off but it had a hold on her and wouldn't let go. The harder she tried to break free of its hold the tighter the grip became.

"There you are," Karmen smiled brightly stepping right in the center of the threesome. "I've been looking for you."

"Is everything okay?" Allen questioned in a calm yet concerned manner as if he was doing absolutely nothing wrong. If Karmen didn't know her husband so well, she would've thought just that.

"The gala is ending shortly and everyone is waiting for you to give your closing remarks."

"Of course. Then we better go," he said taking his wife's hand.

"Don't be rude, Allen. Aren't you going to introduce me to your friends." Karmen kept the same endearing smile on her face as if all was wonderful in the world.

"My apologies. This is Arnold and Crystal and as you both know this is my beautiful wife, Karmen."

"It's a pleasure to meet both of you." Karmen shook both their hands and stared deeply into the eyes of the lady standing in front of her. There was no doubt in Karmen's mind, her husband was fucking that woman.

Chapter Three

Do You Believe In Fairytales

"I heard that the gala was the place to be last night. I was so upset I couldn't make it but by the time my flight got in, you were probably already in bed," Karmen's friend Gayle said as the two ladies sat outside by the pool drinking Mimosas.

"I must say, it was pretty nice. All the guests showed up, seemed to have a great time, and were genuinely happy for him, which was amazing. Allen was being honored and I wanted the night to be perfect for him," Karmen said, before resting her lips on the rim of her glass. She was about to say something else but stopped as her mind drifted off.

Gayle glanced over at her friend who seemed to be in her own world. "Karmen, is everything okay? You seem to be in deep thought?"

"I am. I think Allen is having an affair." Karmen had been forcing herself not to say the words out loud but once she did, she felt a sense of relief.

"Why would you think that? Allen adores you," Gayle stated, surprised by her friend's admission.

"Because I saw him in a conversation with a woman who was exactly his type."

"What type would that be?"

"Hmm...gorgeous."

"Excuse me? You're gorgeous, like drop dead gorgeous. It's actually really annoying. But we've been friends for so long, I just deal with it," Gayle joked. "The first question my son asks me when he comes home from college, after what did I cook of course, is where my hot friend Karmen is. I have to constantly remind him that not only are you married but you're also old enough to be his mother."

"Shut up," Karmen laughed, balling up her napkin and tossing it at her friend. "But seriously, the woman was gorgeous and young."

"Now I'm offended. I thought being in your forties was still young. Isn't the forties suppose to be the new twenties? I don't know about you but I consider myself to be young," Gayle remarked, playing with her tapered bob.

"You know what I mean...she's much younger. Not as young as I was when I first met Allen but she's definitely in her early twenties."

"Okay so he was having a conversation with a younger, hot girl. That doesn't mean they're having an affair."

"It wasn't just the conversation they were having it was the way they were communicating with each other. Then she was wearing this dress. It seemed like the exact sort of dress Allen would pick out."

"Now you're sounding a little paranoid," Gayle said side-eyeing her friend. "You've come to this conclusion because of a dress?"

"I know it might sound crazy to you but I know my husband. In the beginning of our relationship he dressed me for years like I was a doll. He wanted me to look perfect. It wasn't until he was confident that I knew how to dress to his liking did he let me start dressing myself and go shopping on my own."

"That's kinda weird but sexy at the same time," Gayle felt embarrassed to admit.

"Allen is definitely different than most men but that woman Crystal..."

"That's the other woman's name?" Gayle wanted to confirm to make sure she was following the story correctly.

"Yes, he introduced her as Crystal. But only after I put him in a position where he had to. Her entire appearance, from the flawless makeup that wasn't overly done to the way her hair was styled to even the nude polish she was wearing on her nails. Everything screamed Allen. I know my husband is screwing that woman and I'm literally sick to my stomach about it."

"Omigoodness, Karmen. I'm so sorry! I was listening to this thinking you were just being silly and I was trying to be a friend and entertain the silliness but you're serious. Forgive me," Gayle said getting up from her chair and going over to hug her friend.

"It's okay," Karmen laughed trying to hold back her tears.

"No. it's not. What do you want to do...kill him... kill her...kill both of them? I'm your ride or die chick, like the youngin' say. Just let me know how you want to handle this." Now Karmen was laughing for real and Gayle joined in still hugging her friend.

"You really are a mess. But I'm glad you were able to get me to laugh because all I've been wanting to do is cry."

"Don't waste any tears on him. What do you have to cry about? Forget about the fact that with your looks and that body you will have no problem replacing him, but your kids are grown and your husband is beyond loaded. For as long as you all have been married, you might be entitled to even more than half. Of course, I'm not a lawyer but I can refer you to several excellent ones that enjoy, maybe a little too much, taking men like Allen to the cleaners in a divorce."

"That would be extremely helpful if I wasn't still very much in love with my husband."

Gayle sat back down and stared at Karmen. It broke her heart to see her in such pain. "So, let's take divorce off the table. What do you want to do?"

"I want to find out everything I can about this Crystal woman and get her the hell away from my husband, so I can go back to living my fairy-tale life."

Chapter Four

Opposites Attract

Crystal was applying a full face of makeup listening to Big Sean's "I Don't Fuck With You," grinding her hips in the mirror while her best friend Remi posed it up for Snapchat. Today was a free day as she liked to call it. Allen was taking his wife to a formal dinner, so she was hanging out with her bestie. That meant she didn't have to wear an overpriced designer outfit which was more suited for a socialite than a party girl like Crystal. She preferred form fitting dresses, strappy heels, and over the top glam makeup you might see your favorite YouTube Guru do.

"Remi, come zip my dress up!" Crystal screamed out to Remi who was caught in her Snapchat world, not paying her friend any attention.

"Just a sec. I have to post one more snap with this badass view," Remi shouted.

Crystal lived in a sweet Penthouse on Post Oak Blvd in the posh Uptown Houston area. It had every amenity you would expect from an elegant full-service luxury building. The modern Art Deco pad boasted floor-to-ceiling windows, porcelain floors, a gourmet chef's kitchen, and Savant smart home automation. But Crystal's favorite amenities were the starlight infinity edge pool, state-of-the art fitness center, movie theater, private wine room, and stunning skyline views which Remi was currently utilizing for her Snapchat followers. This lavish living was all courtesy of her current sponsor Allen Collins. Crystal literally hit the jackpot with the older yet extremely handsome businessman and she was enjoying all the perks.

"Girl, I posted a pic on Instagram with the skyline and sun setting. Yo, they went crazy. You should see all the likes I got," Remi bragged.

"Just zip up my dress, so we can get outta here."

"You dressed a bit risqué. Don't think mister moneybags would approve," Remi laughed while pulling up the zipper on the white cutout dress.

"I'm off duty tonight, so I can be myself. I get so damn tired of wearing those bougie outfits. I always feel like he's trying to turn me into a replica of his wife. So, annoying," Crystal huffed, rolling her eyes.

"That's what you signed up for. I mean, when he

met you, you came off as a classy, uptown girl."

"I do play the part well," Crystal smiled.

"Yeah, a lil' too well but baby it's worth it," Remi winked.

"Damn straight but it does get hard sometimes maintaining the role. I have to catch myself from slipping. Then I think about this sick ass crib, the Benz in the garage and the hefty allowance I get and I remember super quick." Crystal and Remi both burst out laughing. "Now come on, we have reservations at that new restaurant and we can't be late. The waiting list is ridiculous." Crystal grabbed her purse, keys, and the ladies headed out the door.

"Why aren't I surprised that my big brother is still at the office working. I bet you haven't even had dinner yet," Clayton said to Kasir who seemed to be immersed in some paperwork he was reading through.

"Guilty of both," Kasir remarked. "But the latter is about to be fixed. I'm meeting with a client at that restaurant on Post Oak Blvd."

"You're talking about the new spot."

"Yep." Kasir nodded.

"I'm surprised. That's not really your type of place. A little too trendy."

"I didn't pick the location. I'm meeting with Lance."

"Should've known," Clayton laughed. "I would join you but I have a date of my own. Mine is more for entertainment purposes."

"Of course, it is. Let me guess, you're meeting up with Vannette," Kasir said casually putting the papers he was looking over in his briefcase

"Nope...Margo."

"You're done with Vannette already?"

"No, she's in Miami with Ashton."

"Wow, I'm surprised you let her go."

"I only pretended I wanted her to stay. I knew Margo would be in town for a few days. I needed Vannette out the way," Clayton shrugged.

"The car is downstairs waiting for me and I don't want to be late for my meeting. You enjoy your evening." Kasir patted Clayton on his shoulder as he passed him out the door, then stopped and said, "Don't have too much fun. We're meeting with board members at nine o'clock in the morning. Be on time."

"I know and I'll be there." Clayton watched as his brother headed towards the elevator. Once he was gone, Clayton walked over to his desk. Everything was organized and meticulously in place.

What the hell are you working on, Kasir. Whatever it is, it has you completely engrossed and you've been keeping it a secret, Clayton thought to himself while rummaging through anything he could get his hands on. No matter how hard he searched, Clayton came up empty. *Whatever it is, my brother must've put it in that briefcase he carries everywhere,* he reasoned. Clayton began to tap his fingers on top of the Carpathian, elm, and ebony wood Parnian executive desk, contemplating what he should do next. In the past, he didn't mind taking a backseat and allowing Kasir to be the golden boy but things had changed. After getting a taste of power, Clayton now wanted to take his father's spot at the head of the table. He knew the only way that would happen was to first get rid of his big brother who was next in line.

"What are you up to, Kasir?" Clayton questioned out loud, turning off the lights in his brother's office before making his exit.

"Girl, this place is lit." Remi wiggled her shoulders like she was in a club and ready to dance. "Do you see all the money up in here," she continued, pouring herself another drink.

"I do, but slow down on the champagne. I've almost run through my money for the month. What I have left, has to last me until the first," Crystal remarked. Snatching the bottle from Remi's side of the table.

"Maybe it's time for you to ask for an increase," Remi cracked, steadily looking around trying to find the right kind of trouble to get in.

"Or you can contribute some coins to this high ass bill we 'bout to get hit with," Crystal snapped.

"Don't start actin' up 'cause you on an upward swing right now. Don't forget it was my ass footin' bills and holding us both down when yo' shit had dried up," Remi winked.

Crystal rolled her eyes and pushed the bottle of champagne back over to her bestie. Everything Remi said was spot on. Less than six months ago she was sleeping on Remi's couch, wearing her clothes, and using her cash to get by. Now shit was sweet but Crystal knew with the game she was playing, it could all turn on her in a matter of seconds.

"I think we have a taker," Remi said to Crystal with a sly smile on her face.

"Hello ladies. Can I sit down or are these seats taken?"

Remi glanced over at Crystal. She had that look in her eyes so Crystal knew what was up.

"You can have a seat at our table but anyone who does has to bring a bottle of champagne," Crystal informed him. "Is that going to be a problem?"

"Not a problem at all. I'll have the waiter bring over their best bottle. By the way, my name is Lance."

"I'm Crystal and this is my friend, Remi."

"Nice to meet you lovely ladies. Excuse me while I go order that bottle. I'll be back shortly."

"I told you we had a taker!" Remi grinned widely.

"You could always spot 'em. I'm just glad we can keep the bubbly flowing on someone else's dime," Crystal sighed with relief.

"Let's just hope he isn't into threesomes since it's only one of him and two of us," Remi smacked. "Not in the sharing mood."

"Seems you spoke too soon. I think he's bringing company." Crystal raised an eyebrow.

"Ladies, the waiter will be bringing the bottle over shortly," Lance said. "Hope you don't mind but a business associate of mine will be joining us."

"We don't mind, but another guest means another bottle," Crystal smiled.

"Tell you what. I'll simply cover the bill, so we don't have to waste any more time discussing who's paying for what," Lance stated.

"Works for me," Crystal said.

"What about you?" Lance looked over at Remi.

"I'm good," Remi said, putting her glass down. She was waiting for the new bottle to arrive so she could refill it.

"Great! How rude of me, this is Kasir. Kasir, meet Crystal and Remi."

"Hello," Kasir said in a short almost cold tone. He didn't even look in the women's direction, instead keeping his attention on Lance. "We're supposed to be discussing business. Not wasting time having drinks with some random women."

Crystal and Remi locked eyes, slightly giggling. They found the tall, handsome man dressed in a designer suit, perfectly manicured hands, with the clean cut and thin mustache amusing.

"Relax. We have to eat," Lance said to Kasir in his typical upbeat tone. "First dinner then business." He patted Kasir's arm and sat down.

Kasir reluctantly took a seat, not hiding his discontentment. He knew he should've insisted Lance meet at his office but he was a very valuable client, so he agreed to do the bullshit dinner thing. Lance was the founder and CEO of Reps Up. A one stop fitness facility, specializing in giving members access to nutrition specialists, personal trainers, and an individualized regimen to meet each person's needs. Initially, it was a startup company that no one believed in but Lance, since the market was flooded with gyms. But he had a vision. After coming up with a proposal he was able to convince Allen Collins to become an investor and Lance became the company's first client.

Soon Reps Up went from a small startup to a lucrative franchise with locations all across the United States. Now Lance had plans to take the franchise international and the Collins family wanted to make sure they remained in the loop. Due to the continued success of the business, Allen Collins had been able to clean millions of dollars in drug money and he had no intentions of letting that end. Which was the only reason Kasir hadn't got up and walked out the restaurant. Lance was a genius at branding and creating a money-spinning corporation with his intense work ethic but he enjoyed playing just as hard. He loved women and partying and for Kasir those were afterthoughts. You'd think, Clayton would be a better fit but Lance always insisted working directly with Kasir. He respected the fact Kasir was all about the bottom line...money.

"It seems your business associate has taken a liking to my friend," Crystal remarked to Kasir.

"For the moment," Kasir replied dryly.

"I guess men like you and Lance can only have short-term interest in random women like us, huh." Crystal's comment caught Kasir off guard.

"You weren't supposed to hear that," Kasir admitted, looking over at Crystal for the first time. He wasn't expecting her to be so pretty. Her makeup was a bit too heavy for his taste and the dress a tad too tight but appealing nonetheless.

"You haven't glanced in my direction since sitting down and now you can't stop staring at me, what gives?"

"I apologize. Not only for staring but also for the random women comment. It was inappropriate."

"More like offensive, rude."

"I suppose you're right."

"I'm messing with you," Crystal laughed, nudging Kasir on his shoulder. "You really do need to relax. I found what you said to be very amusing."

"Amusing." Kasir nodded his head. "I don't believe any woman has every used the word amusing to describe me."

"Not surprising. Most women would probably throw out words like uptight, a bit tense but I can see through all that. The first thing you need to do is have a drink." Crystal began pouring Kasir a glass of champagne.

"I'm good on the drink." Kasir pushed the glass away.

"Look at them." Crystal pointed her finger in Lance and Remi's direction. "They're talking, laughing and clearly enjoying each other's company which means for at least the next hour, you're stuck with me. Don't make me walk away from this table because if I do, Remi will follow. I don't think that would please your business partner very much and obviously his happiness is important to you."

"Why do you think that?" Kasir questioned.

"Because if his happiness wasn't important to you, you would've already left. Now are you having that drink or not?"

"Fill it up."

"My pleasure," Crystal smiled.

Kasir unwittingly found himself smiling back at the young beauty. Only minutes ago, she was nowhere on his radar but now had his full attention. Kasir wasn't used to being drawn to a woman like Crystal. He preferred women who were more aloof, elegant, and conservative in their appearance. Crystal on the other hand was representing for the sexy, over the top, party girls. The sort of look Kasir would normally frown upon, but it seemed at least for tonight, opposites attracting was in full effect.

Chapter Five

Where You Wanna Be

Ashton was dancing seductively in front of the exotic, European pool as if the nightclub was devoid of anyone else but her. A combination of expensive wine and party pills had Ashton in her own world. She seemed to be making love to herself as her body gyrated to the hip hop beat blasting from the sound system. She had a glass in one hand while the other glided across the silk material caressing her body, as she fondled her breasts before slightly rising up the side of the dress over her right hip. Ashton was about to give every man in the club a hard on without even trying.

The poolside ambiance mixed with the nightclub's decadent vibe was very enticing for the rich, famous, and beautiful people in Miami Beach. One rich man in particular had zoomed in on Ashton from one of the lavish private cabanas that offered voyeuristic views.

"Stay here. I'll be back," Damacio said leaving the cabana, headed in Ashton's direction. He took his time walking near her, as he was enjoying the sensual show she was putting on. "Hello," Damacio said evenly.

"Hi." Ashton's eyes remained closed while she continued to dance and her tone was almost breathless.

"Why don't you come to my cabana and sit with me."

"Do I look like I wanna sit down?" Ashton twirled around, giggling.

"The club is closing soon. I would really like to talk to you before that happens." Damacio gently put his hand around Ashton's slim waist, to slow her down.

"Why are you touching me?" she opened her eyes and asked. "You really shouldn't waste your time. You're not my type."

"Really? Why is that?"

"I like my men dark and I don't mean dark hair and dark eyes," Ashton smiled.

"I have time to waste, so I'll take my chances." Damacio continued to rest his hand around Ashton's waist. He was tempted to pull her in close because although her mouth was saying one thing, her eyes were saying something else.

"I need some more wine. Excuse me while I go look

for my friends." Ashton slipped away from Damacio's grasp.

"I'll come with you."

"Suit yourself," she giggled again as Damacio followed behind her, loving the chase.

When Ashton went back inside the club to the booth they were seating at, no one was there. "What the fuck!?"

"Are you sure this is the table?" Damacio questioned.

"I'm tipsy not drunk," Ashton sniped. "I can't believe they left me," she said reaching in her purse to get her cell phone. "Fuck! My phone died."

"I can take you wherever you want to go," Damacio offered.

Ashton didn't say a word. Instead she headed back outside towards the parking lot and Damacio was once again trailing right behind her. She was looking around to see if the rental car they came in was still there but it wasn't. At this point, Ashton's adrenaline was rushing, the alcohol and pills were kicking in and the five inch heels she was wearing were killing her feet.

"Baby, yo' fine ass needs to come home wit' me," some muscular built dude who resembled a football player came up to Ashton and said.

"Gosh, I need to sit down," Ashton mumbled, starting to feel dizzy.

"I got you babe," the man said before Damacio cut him off.

"She's with me." Damacio took Ashton's arm and pulled her close.

"Man, step back! She ain't fuckin' wit' you like that." The powerful built man got up in Damacio's space. Before he could say another word, he was surrounded by a small army of men with guns aimed to his head.

"Oh shit! Who the fuck are you?!" Ashton eyes widened. "Yo, this shit is messing with my high."

"I suggest you move," Damacio warned the man, who was more than willing to take his advice. All he was trying to do was take a pretty girl home with him and maybe get some pussy but not die in the process.

"My bad. I didn't realize she was wit' you. No disrespect." The man bolted with the quickness. Damacio's security didn't put away their weapons until he had gotten in his car and drove away. This left Damacio right where he wanted to be, holding Ashton.

"So, can I give you that ride?" he asked.

"Just as long as you don't kill me," Ashton stared up at him and said.

"Never." All the chasing paid off, Damacio thought as he took Ashton's hand and led her to his awaiting car.

What Kasir figured would only be an hour conversation to bide time, ended up being three. When Lance was ready to leave the restaurant, Kasir wanted to stay. His conversation with Crystal started off as lighthearted, then it became deep with a mixture of laughter. It was the right combination to keep Kasir glued to every word

Crystal said. They were now finishing up their second bottle of champagne and neither wanted the night to end.

"Do you regret staying here with me instead of leaving with Lance?" Crystal asked.

"Nope. How about you. Do you wish you would've left with your girlfriend instead of being here with me?"

"As a matter of fact..." Crystal smiled.

"Don't even try it!" Kasir cut her off. They both started laughing. "Honestly, I can't remember the last time I enjoyed a woman's company this much," he admitted.

"I'm sure you're surprised. Especially with me being some random chick and all."

"Wow, you're never going to let me live that down. I said I was sorry." Kasir shook his head.

"I'm only kidding. I forgive you." Crystal put her hand on top of Kasir's and stroked it softly.

"I don't believe you."

"I can show you better than I can tell you."

"You sure?"

"Positive." Crystal sipped down the last of her champagne. "Let's get outta here before I change my mind."

Kasir gulped down the rest of his drink and rushed out with Crystal. They had the perfect buzz. Intoxicated enough to make rash decisions but not so far gone they wouldn't be able to remember every detail of the incredible sex they were about to have.

"I thought my apartment was nice. This place is incredible," Crystal commented as she was ripping off Kasir's clothes.

"Not as incredible as your body. That dress you were wearing didn't do you justice. Luckily it was easy to take off."

"Easy access, baby!" Crystal teased pushing Kasir down on his bed. Not giving him an opportunity to take control, she had his rock hard dick in her wet mouth on some deep throat shit.

"Damn!" Kasir moaned over and over again, not ready for the tongue and pussy tricks a seasoned pro like Crystal was about to put on him. Kasir was far from a virgin and engaged in plenty of sex he had considered amazing until tonight. Once she slid her toned, curvy body on top of him and straddled Kasir like a stallion, he was hooked.

"You feel so good," Crystal called out breathlessly as Kasir pressed his hands into her ass, wanting to go as deep inside as possible to feel all her wetness. He grabbed the back of her hair, pulling Crystal near, so his mouth could taste her nipples. She closed her eyes, savoring the tingling sensation going through her entire body. Kasir and Crystal had what each would describe as immaculate sex all night.

Chapter Six

The Thrill Factor

"Oh, Maria, muchacha hermosa," Alejo cooed, picking up his granddaughter who was sitting in her highchair. He lifted her above his head and smiled widely as she laughed happily. "For your next birthday, I'll buy you an Irish thoroughbred," he said proudly.

"Daddy, she's too young for a horse," Maria's mother, Aleta, said.

"No, no...never too young for a prized pony. My granddaughter shall have it all, just like her mother did. Now all I need is a grandson."

"Mr. Hernandez, can I speak with you for a moment?" Gilberto, one of his men came in the room and asked.

"Don't you see me spending time with my granddaughter. Do not disturb me." Alejo stated angrily.

"My apologies, sir." Gilberto bowed his head. "You told me to let you know when the phone call you were waiting for was received."

"Yes. I'll be right there," Alejo told his worker before signaling him to leave. "Tu abuelo, will be back shortly, mi amor," he kissed his granddaughter sweetly and handed Maria to her mother then left the room.

Alejo walked on the rich mahogany floors, down the long hall at his 3-story contemporary Mediterranean waterfront villa. "I'll take the phone call outside," he said stepping out on one of the covered terraces that had unobstructed panoramic views to Biscayne Bay, Key Biscayne, and Downtown skyline.

"As you wish." Gilberto handed the phone to his boss.

"I hear you're looking to take over the Houston drug territory. I believe I can be of great assistance to you," Alejo stated confidently and with good reason.

Houston is one of the most significant cocaine and marijuana distribution centers in the United States. Large quantities are distributed from Houston to numerous market areas, including Atlanta, Chicago, Miami, and New Orleans. Alejo Hernandez's affiliation to a powerful Mexican Cartel allowed him to be the primary source of any drug that needed to be supplied.

For many years, Allen Collins dominated the southeastern drug market due to his longstanding relationship with Alejo. Their association allowed both men to accumulate an exorbitant amount of money but now Alejo was ready for that partnership to come to an end. He felt in recent years that Allen had gotten beside himself, thinking he was better than him because of his success in the corporate world. Allen Collins was a respected legitimate businessman in the city of Houston and it infuriated Alejo. He wanted to humble the great man and figured the best way to accomplish that was to take away what brought him his power...drug money.

"I need a mimosa and an Excedrin," Ashton mumbled as she walked out the bedroom, rubbing her eyes. When she was halfway down the hall, she started to question her whereabouts. "Where am, I?" she asked out loud, glancing around. It wasn't until she stumbled into the living room did she realize where that was.

"Ashton, let me get you something to put on!" Damacio jumped up, taking off his V-neck t-shirt in the process. "Here, take this."

"Calm down. I'm sure you and your friends have seen a naked woman before," Ashton shrugged, thinking it was no big deal to prance around in her birthday suit.

Ashton wasn't concerned but Damacio was livid. He knew the two men sitting in his living room were probably ready to bust a nut as they sat lusting over her. "Please, just put this on," Damacio implored.

"Fine," Ashton said casually, slipping the t-shirt

over her head. "Now can I get that mimosa and Excedrin?"

"Sure. Follow me to the kitchen."

"Is this your place?" Ashton questioned, taking her three fingers to massage the side of her head.

"Yes, it is. Do you always walk around naked?" Damacio wanted to know, quickly changing the subject.

"Only first thing in the morning and before I go to bed since I sleep naked. Honestly when I woke up, I thought I was in my hotel room. I had no idea I was at your place. I guess I did have too much to drink last night."

"It was more than having too much to drink. Mixing drugs with alcohol is never a good mix," Damacio reasoned.

"What makes you think I was doing drugs?" she asked, sitting down on one of the chairs in the kitchen.

"Let's just say, I've been on the Miami party scene long enough to know when someone has mixed drugs and booze."

"I only popped a couple pills. It's harmless. Do you have a phone charger I can use?" Now Ashton wanted to change the subject.

"Yeah, I'll get it for you after I pour you some orange juice."

"Don't forget to add the champagne. I asked for a mimosa not plain OJ."

"I really think you should eat something before having alcohol," Damacio suggested. He was finding it difficult giving Ashton advice without staring at her long bare legs. She had them crossed and the fresh French pedicure only further highlighted her smooth caramel colored skin. What he found most attractive was she seemed to be oblivious to just how beautiful she was.

"Fine, I'll have one of those bagels," she said noticing them on the kitchen counter. "Can you toast it and add butter for me…thanks."

Damacio found himself laughing at her request. He wasn't used to people asking him to do things for them, he was used to being served. "So, what do you do for a living, Ashton?" Damacio asked while putting the bagel in the toaster.

"I'm in college."

"You have very expensive taste for a college girl."

"How do you know that?"

"When we got here last night, you tossed your dress and shoes on the floor. When I picked them up I was familiar with the designers. I have a sister with very expensive taste," Damacio smirked.

"Yes, I do have expensive taste. Luckily, I have a daddy who enjoys spoiling me."

"So, you have one of those."

"What's one of those?"

"A sugar daddy."

Ashton let out a loud laugh. "I like young cute guys, not old rich ones. When I said daddy, I was speaking of the one who actually participated in giving me life," she cracked.

"My apologies. I hope I didn't offend you."

"Not at all. It takes a lot to offend me. My bagel's ready," Ashton pointed to the toaster. "Since you're so interested in what I do, let's talk about what you do. I wasn't so drunk last night, that I forgot your bodyguards or whoever they were, pulled out their guns ready to kill for you. What was that about?"

"I guess there's some people who are willing to do anything to make sure I stay alive," Damacio said, handing Ashton the bagel and mimosa.

"Interesting." She bit down on the bagel, dangling her leg, amused by Damacio's response.

"Do you go to college here in Miami?"

"No, I go to school in Houston. I'm in Miami for my spring break. I plan to party hard for the next week."

"I know I'm not your type but do you think maybe we can have dinner while you're in town?"

"Before I answer, let me clarify one thing. Because I said you weren't my type, doesn't mean I don't find you attractive. You standing there with no shirt on, I had no idea your body was so cut," Ashton smiled.

"I'm glad you approve."

"I do but I'll have to pass on dinner," she said taking a sip of her mimosa.

Damacio's face frowned up before asking, "Why?"

"I came here to party with my girlfriends not to have dinner with some guy."

"I see." Damacio nodded his head.

"Can you get that charger for me. I need a ride to get back to my hotel."

"I'll get the charger but one of my men will take you wherever you need to go," Damacio told her.

"Thank you. Do you mind if I take a shower before I go?"

"Of course not."

"Great and I hope there's no hard feelings because I declined your dinner invitation."

"None at all," Damacio lied.

"Cool. Off to the shower I go," Ashton smiled before disappearing down the hall.

Damacio felt a twinge of anger, frustration, mixed with a thrill factor. He was used to women pursuing him. Damacio couldn't even remember the last time he approached a woman. Yet Ashton had no problem shutting him down and it turned him on. The idea of having to chase a woman he was so drawn to gave him a rush that had been lacking in his personal life. Damacio had no intention of giving up on Ashton, in fact he was only getting started.

Chapter Seven

Can't Have Everything

"I thought you were in for the night," Karmen said to her husband as he was fixing his tie. She was standing in front of the vanity mirror moisturizing her hands watching him.

"That was my plan but I forgot I had a dinner meeting tonight," Allen told his wife.

"Why don't you have Kasir or Clayton handle the meeting."

"I won't be gone long." He came over and kissed his wife on the cheek. "That's my favorite negligee. It always looks beautiful on you," he commented admiring the antique lavender, Chantilly lace trim satin slip with a deep plunging neckline.

"I know. That's why I put it on," she turned to her husband and said who was on his way out the bedroom door. "Allen, please don't go. Stay home with me tonight." Karmen's voice had a pleading tone to it.

"I would love to but I really have to go. I promise not to stay out late. Love you." Allen blew a kiss to his wife and went about his business, unaware she knew damn well the only meeting he had was with his mistress.

Karmen prayed she could avoid this but her husband was leaving her no choice. For her own sanity, she needed concrete proof her husband was cheating and she planned on getting it.

"Hello, this is Randall Finch," he announced as if to confirm to callers that they had reached the correct person.

"Hi Randall. This is Karmen Collins. We spoke about a week ago."

"Yes, you had some suspicions regarding your husband."

"I still do and I need to have those suspicions confirmed. Are you available?"

"Yes, I am."

"How soon can you start?"

"Whenever you're ready, Mrs. Collins."

"I'm ready now. Can you start tonight?"

"I sure can. If you give me his cell phone number, I can start tracking him as we speak."

"Good because my husband is on the move right now and I need to know if he's with another woman."

Karmen gave the private investigator her husband's cell number and the other information he requested. Her best friend Gayle recommended him. She was adamant he was the best in the business and she took her at her word. Initially, Karmen was reluctant to hire a private investigator, as she didn't want to invade on her husband's privacy but that had changed. She wanted to save her marriage and the longer she allowed an affair to go on, the closer her husband would get to the other woman, at least that's how Karmen rationalized it.

For the last hour, Kasir was debating whether or not to call Lance. Although they had hung out a few times together, for Kasir it was always about business, the fun was strictly to appease one of the firm's elite clients. But he couldn't hold out any longer.

"My man, Kasir. What's good?" Lance answered.

"Are you busy?"

"What kinda question is that. I'm never too busy for you. I do hope this call isn't about the other night. I know it was supposed to be a dinner meeting but I got sidetracked. Beautiful women have a tendency to do that to me," he laughed.

"Actually, it is about the other night."

"My bad, man. It won't..."

"Listen," Kasir cut Lance off before he started on one of his apologetic rants. "I'm trying to get in touch with the young lady, Crystal, who was at the table with us."

"Oh, Remi's friend. So, you liked her." Kasir could see Lance smiling through the phone. "She is sexy but I didn't think she was your type. Let me find out you're crossing over to the other side."

"Slow down. It's nothing like that. There was some business I wanted to discuss with her," Kasir lied. It was making him uncomfortable at the level of amusement Lance was having at his expense.

"I don't think you and Crystal are in the same line of business but if you say so. I can put a call to Remi and get her number for you."

"No, just give Remi my number and tell her to have Crystal call me at her earliest convenience. She may not want me to have her number," Kasir said, trying to make it sound completely professional.

"Trust me, I'm sure Crystal would love for you to have her number. You're one of the most eligible bachelors in Houston. I know...I know, this is strictly business but I'm just saying," Lance remarked.

"I appreciate you doing this for me, Lance. I'm about to head into this meeting but let's reschedule our dinner soon. Talk to you later."

Kasir knew exactly where his conversation with Lance was headed and he wasn't interested. He hated that he needed to get him involved but desperation got the best of him. After having the best sex of his life, when he woke up in the morning, Crystal was gone. He was hoping she would call him but quickly remembered they exchanged everything except numbers. No matter how hard Kasir tried, he couldn't stop replaying his sex session with Crystal or how good it felt being inside her. Now all he could do was wait and for Kasir, who preferred to control every aspect of a situation, this would prove to be a difficult task.

"I'm glad you were able to make it," Crystal said giving Allen a kiss when she let him in. Although he had a key, he would always knock first which she appreciated. It made Crystal feel like he respected her.

"Me too. I wasn't sure I would be able to but it worked out."

"That's all that matters," she said kissing him on the lips. So, can I get you something to drink."

"Yes, a drink would be nice."

"Your regular?"

"Of course," Allen stated. It was mandatory for Crystal to keep a 2005 bottle of Chateau Petrus in stock at all times. Luckily, Allen foot the bill, and all she had to do was make sure nobody touched it but him.

"How's your day been going so far?" Crystal asked trying to make small talk. They had been seeing each other for over three months but she still struggled to have a conversation with Allen. Mainly because Crystal was scared if she talked too much, he would realize she was a hoodrat. "Here you go," she smiled handing Allen the glass of wine."

"Thank you. My day's been hectic as usual. This is

the first time I had a chance to unwind."

"Well, relax. I promise to take good care of you." Crystal sat on his knee and crossed her slender legs.

"I noticed that dress over on the couch. It's rather tasteless," Allen commented, resting his hand on Crystal's thigh. "I hope you didn't go out wearing that."

"Of course not! My friend Remi left it over here. She's supposed to be stopping by to pick it up. That's why I have it on the couch," Crystal lied. The dress Allen was speaking of, was the hoochie mama attire she wore the other night when she went to the restaurant with Remi. It was actually on her couch because she had been sniffing it nonstop since Kasir's scent was all over it, which she loved.

"Good. I was concerned for a minute. I couldn't imagine you wearing such cheap clothes."

"Baby, you know that isn't my style. Why would I wear something like that when you buy me the most beautiful clothes? Enough about that, I want to make you feel good."

Crystal got on her knees and began to take off Allen's belt and unbutton his pants. She knew putting his dick in her mouth would shut him up and end his interrogation. She really did enjoy pleasuring Allen but he always made her feel so inadequate. He was the cream of the crop and only through masterful manipulation was a woman like Crystal able to enter his circle and it kept her on edge. The only time she felt she could even the playing field was in the bed, so Crystal did her best to keep him there.

Randall Finch was parked in front of the high-rise luxury building, sitting patiently in his black Chevrolet Tahoe. Based on the tracking device and locating Allen Collins' car in the parking garage, Randall Finch was confident that his client's husband was in the building. After a couple of hours, the star of the show finally revealed his face. Allen Collins exited out the building alone but Randall still took pictures. It would've been ideal if he could've gotten photos with Allen and his mistress but Randall wasn't concerned. He was willing to bet money that this was where he kept the other woman stashed. Now all Randall had to do was prove it.

Chapter Eight

Whenever... Wherever

"Another night, another club!" Ashton cheered while she, Vannette, and a couple of their other friends danced in the VIP section. For the past four nights, it had been an endless party for the ladies. The only time they chilled was to sleep, shower, and dress. They barely even ate. Their diet consisted of champagne, pills, and empty calorie snacks but they were having the time of their lives.

"Oh wow, look who just came into the VIP section." Vannette nudged Ashton's arm.

"Who?" Ashton asked but was barely paying attention because she was digging in her purse for one of her party pills.

"It's Shanice Monroe but she goes by Beautiful Hershey Chocolate on Instagram."

"So." Ashton shrugged, not interested in the least.

"She's an Instagram model. She got like a ton of followers after D-Boy commented on one of her pics and started following her."

"You talking about the Houston rapper D-Boy?" Ashton question.

"Duh! She's always posting photos with her and rappers, athletes, and even some actors. That guy she's with must be rolling in dough, because she only fucks with ballers or so I heard."

"Vannette, like who cares about some Instagram thot. You sound so stupid right now," Ashton rolled her eyes, grabbing a bottle of water to wash down her pill.

"That's easy for you to say. Your family is so loaded you'll never have to work a day in your life. I'm trying to get my come up. So, of course I follow chicks like Shanice. She's going to point you in the direction of all the rich men."

"Do what you gotta do."

"Yeah, especially since we both know your brother isn't settling down anytime soon," Vannette popped.

"Definitely don't waste your time on him. I think Clayton is too in love with himself to ever settle down. Plus, he's such an asshole why would you even want to. Girl, are you still club stalking that chick?" Ashton glanced over in the direction Vannette was staring.

"No, I'm drooling over the guy she's with. That man is fine. I bet he's rich too."

"Omigosh!" Ashton belted.

"What's wrong?"

"That's the guy I was telling you about," she huffed. A surge of jealousy hit Ashton like a ton of bricks and it had her shook. The girl was standing up, gyrating in front of Damacio as he sat on the couch watching her.

"You mean the one who took you back to his place after the club a few nights ago?"

"Yes!"

"What the hell! You didn't tell me he was that fuckin' hot. You lucky, bitch! Did you fuck him?"

"No, I didn't," Ashton snapped.

"Why not?" Vannette gave her friend a baffled stare.

"I wasn't in the mood for sex. I just wanted to get back to the hotel and sleep in my room."

"You're crazy! I guess that's what happens when men are constantly trying to get with you...you start taking them for granted. Because there is no way that fine motherfucker wouldn't have been inside of me," Vannette nodded.

"Whatever, I need a drink. I'll be back."

"We have a bottle of champagne right here!" Vannette called out but Ashton had already stormed off.

Ashton why are you so upset? He's not your man. You barely even know him, so why do you feel like going over and scratching his eyes out for coming to the club with another woman, Ashton thought to herself as she

54

walked over to the bar. The only reason she stormed off was because she didn't want Vannette or the other girls to see how upset she was. They were used to Ashton being the ice queen but she was on the verge of a meltdown and she couldn't even figure out why.

"Can I buy you a drink? Or better yet, get you a mimosa." Ashton heard a familiar voice say, shaking her out of her thoughts.

"I'm good." She turned around and saw Damacio standing in front of her.

"You don't look good."

"Excuse me?!"

"You don't look good...you look upset but still beautiful."

"I'm not upset."

"Are you sure? Look at me." Damacio lifted up Ashton's face. "I see you've been doing drugs again."

"I told you, it's just pills."

"It's still drugs, Ashton."

Ashton tried to move her face away but Damacio maintained a firm hold. "I'm not done talking to you."

"I'm sure your date is wondering where you are, so maybe you should go."

"That's why you're upset, because you saw me come in with another woman."

"Please!" Ashton scoffed but her eyes were telling a different story and she knew it, so she quickly switched things up. "I don't care who you're with, just like I'm sure you don't care who I'm with."

Ashton's eyes went from being filled with jealousy to seeking some harmless payback. She walked over to a guy who had been staring her down the entire time she was at the bar and asked him to dance.

Damacio didn't move. He stood watching Ashton make love to the music while some man put his hands all over her. Now it was his turn to be on the receiving end of jealousy and Damacio wasn't handling it well at all. He stood watching Ashton play seductively with her hair as she pressed her body against the man. After a few more seconds, he'd had enough.

"What the fuck are you doing!" Damacio grabbed Ashton's arm, holding her tightly.

"Motherfucker, you betta back up!" the guy Ashton had been dancing with roared.

"You need to stay outta this!" Damacio warned.

"Who the fuck you think you talkin' to?! I'll lay yo'..."

Before he could spit out another word, Damacio's fist had connected with the man's face and he was on the floor.

"What have you done?!" Ashton gasped.

The man's friends started running towards the dance floor but Damacio's shooters were armed and ready, waiting on their asses. Damacio left them to deal with the raucous he started while he yanked Ashton off the floor.

"I can't believe you did that," Ashton said looking back to see what was going on.

"Isn't that what you wanted...to piss me the fuck off! Well it worked."

"You started it! Coming here with some Instagram thot and letting her dance all over you!"

"You were jealous. Is that so hard for you to admit? Answer me!" Damacio demanded.

"Why do you care so fuckin' much!" Ashton yelled.

"Because I want you." Damacio pulled Ashton close and started kissing her. At first, she resisted but his lips were too soft, wet, and satisfying. She kissed him even harder with more passion. In a matter of seconds, Damacio had her against the wall. They were ready to undress each other right in the club.

"We better stop before they throw us out," Ashton said between kisses.

"They can't. I own it," Damacio replied, putting his tongue down her neck.

"We can't do this here," she said breathlessly.

"Then come home with me. We can leave now."

"I can't. I don't..."

Damacio put his index finger over Ashton's lips not letting her say another word. "No more games. You're leaving with me, now. You understand?"

Ashton simply nodded her head yes. At that moment, she would've followed Damacio anywhere he wanted to go.

Chapter Nine

Decisions...Decisions....

"I think yesterday's meeting was a success. I wouldn't be surprised if Gordon called later on today and let us be the primary investor of their new business," Clayton walked into Kasir's office and said.

"I agree but I doubt it will be today. More like Friday."

"You think he'll wait that long?" Clayton asked.

"I'm positive," Kasir nodded. "Gordon knows we're very interested and would be the best fit for his business but he's also greedy. If he bites too soon, he thinks we'll ask for a larger percentage, which of course he doesn't want to give. But I've already ran the numbers so I know what we need for it be beneficial to our bottom line and it's a lot less than what Gordon thinks," Kasir stated, sizing up Gordon and his game plan. He was confident with his assessment.

"Seems you have it all figured out," Clayton said deciding to sit down.

"Don't I always," Kasir casually commented as he checked his phone. "It's the reason our numbers keep going up each year, when everyone else is struggling to figure out what they need to do to keep from going under."

"True indeed. You always have the answers, big brother." Clayton's sarcasm went unnoticed by Kasir because he was more interested in the text message on his phone. "Don't you find it odd dad wasn't at the meeting yesterday?" Clayton questioned, wanting his brother's full attention.

"Ummm…" There was a long pause as Kasir replied to the text.

"What has you so occupied over there?" Clayton wanted to know.

"Just something I'm working on but in regard to our father, the meeting was very late in the day. He probably didn't feel like coming back to the office after he left."

"You don't find that strange? Workaholic isn't a strong enough word to describe dad's hunger for business but the last few months, he's been off. This is the third meeting in the last few months he's blown off."

Kasir let what Clayton said sink in for a minute. "I

hadn't really thought about it but now that you mention it, he hasn't been as focused on business lately." Kasir put his left elbow on top of his desk and rested his hand on his chin as in deep thought.

"Personally, I think something is going on with our father." Clayton spoke up and said, irritated with Kasir's long silence.

"Do you think he's sick? Maybe we should ask mom if dad has some sort of medical condition he's keeping from us."

"I don't think he's ill," Clayton scoffed.

"Then what?"

"I don't know but whatever it is, has him preoccupied. Besides our outside business, we're trying to build and maintain a multimillion dollar corporation. We can't afford to have a CEO who isn't involved. You might need to step up and take over, Kasir," Clayton implied.

"Take over...you mean as CEO?"

"Yes."

"Hold on, let's not get ahead of ourselves." Kasir put down his phone and stood up. "A. C. Enterprise is dad's baby. He started this company because he wanted to have a legitimate business to leave to his children."

"Exactly. It's supposed to be his legacy that we carry on. That won't happen if our father neglects the family business. We can't let that happen."

"And it won't. Missing a few meetings and..."

"Extremely important meetings," Clayton clarified.

"Yes, extremely important but it doesn't justify

ousting our father from his own company," Kasir made clear.

"Maybe you're right but you always stress the importance of being two steps ahead. Recognizing a potential complication and coming up with a solution before it becomes a problem. Those are your words or are you forgetting because the complication is our dad?"

"You do have a valid point," Kasir acknowledged. "I will admit, I'm somewhat surprised you seem so willing to allow me to be dad's predecessor."

"It's no secret you're next in line to run the company as you should be. Although we're only a couple years apart in age, as you stated, you're the one who always has everything figured out. You know this business inside and out."

"All that might be true but until dad says he's ready to step down, he is still CEO. We'll keep an eye on things and if there is cause for concern, we'll address it." Kasir made his position clear and for him the discussion was over.

"I had some concerns and wanted to bring it to your attention but I think you're right. I appreciate you listening," Clayton nodded.

"Of course. Now that we got that out the way, let's discuss the merger..."

Clayton pretended to be listening to what his brother was saying but he was actually strategizing his next move. Kasir would never admit it but Clayton knew the idea of being in control of A. C. Enterprise had his brother salivating at the mouth which was his plan. He purposely put the idea of being CEO in Kasir's mind, although Clayton had no intentions of ever letting that happen.

"Mrs. Collins, please come in," Randall said, pulling out a chair for her to sit down.

"Please, call me Karmen," she smiled.

"Karmen, I'm glad you were able to come by on such short notice."

"You said it was important, I wanted to oblige you."

"Then I'll get right to it." Randall reached in his top drawer and pulled out a large envelope. He took out several photos. First, showing Allen Collins coming out of the high-rise apartment building. He followed that up with photos of Crystal. Some of her inside the apartment building and others of her coming out.

Karmen scrutinized the photos intently. "The photos of my husband are from the day I hired you, correct?"

"Yes, it is. Unfortunately, I wasn't able to get pictures of them together but I've gathered enough information that I believe proves this is the woman your husband is having an affair with."

Karmen didn't need any convincing but she wanted the private investigator to give her all the information he had. "Please, continue."

"Your husband owns a condo in that building. It's under A. C. Enterprise and it's listed as a corporate apartment. Crystal Anderson is the tenant listed on the apartment."

"How long has she been living there?" Karmen wanted to know.

"Three months."

"I see." Karmen stood up from the chair, then paced the floor before stopping and leaning against the wall. She put her head down for a few seconds and although he tried, Randall couldn't stop himself from staring at the stunner. Karmen had on a simple blue, soft, and stretchy jersey jumpsuit. It had a surplice neckline bodice with pleats on the wide leg silhouette. She complimented her look with Yves Saint Laurent ultra-sleek ankle strap stilettos in a neutral hue. Her makeup was subtle with minimum jewelry, and it was her natural beauty that truly stood out.

"Can I get you something to drink?" Randall offered becoming concerned. He could see how distraught she was even though she was doing an excellent job of holding it together.

"No, I'm fine." Karmen sat back down and once again studied the photos.

"I apologize in advance if you feel like I'm out of line but I must say I didn't expect for you to be so beautiful," Randall said coyly.

"What, you expected me to look like a frumpy housewife?"

"Yes, I did," he admitted with embarrassment. "Looking at you, I can't imagine why your husband or any man for that matter would cheat on you."

"I'm sure you've been a private investigator long

enough to know, most of the time, cheating has nothing to do with how someone looks."

"Touché. Again, I apologize if you feel disrespected in any way by what I said."

"Randall, the only person who owes me an apology is my husband."

"Does that mean you're going to confront your husband with the information I've given you?"

"Not yet. I want you to continue following my husband and also, I want you to find out everything you can about Crystal Anderson."

"I can do that, if you wish but I want you to be sure."

"Sure, about what?"

"You want me to dig even deeper. The more you know, the stronger your resentment will become towards your husband and the other woman. I would hate for this to turn into another Clara Harris tragedy. I don't think you would hold up well in prison," Randall reasoned.

"Trust me, I have no intentions of going to jail for killing my husband or his mistress. What I do plan on doing is gathering all the ammunition I can before making a move. I'm expecting you to do your job and be very thorough while doing so."

"Enough said. I'm on it. I guess the same way I had underestimated your beauty I also underestimated your strength. I won't make that mistake again." Randall continued tapping the pen on his desk as he spoke to Karmen while trying to size her up at the same time.

"Good." Karmen stood up and shook Randall's hand. "Thank you for the information you've provided thus far. I look forward to you getting the rest."

"Whatever I can do to help. I'll keep you updated with any new developments," Randall promised.

"Thank you." Karmen maintained her stoic aura until she made it to her car. "You sonofabitch!" she shrieked, finally breaking down while sitting her car. She banged her hands on the stirring wheel, wishing she could rip it off. If she continued to tap into her anger, she probably could.

Karmen had suspected Allen was stepping out on her but suspecting and your suspicions being confirmed were two different things. She could no longer pretend to be in denial or make excuses for her husband's un-explained whereabouts or late nights working at the office or plain bullshit excuses Allen kept pulling out of his ass. Her husband was a cheater and Karmen had to decide whether she wanted to fight for her marriage, or leave the man she has loved for her entire adult life.

Chapter Ten

Until We Meet Again

"My son finally decides to show his face. If you weren't my favorite child, I would've cut you off years ago," Alejo said before kissing Damacio on his forehead.

"Father, I apologize. I've been extremely busy with work." Damacio explained taking a seat on the large hardwood design L-shaped crocodile leather sectional.

"When is running around clubs, partying with celebrities work?" Alejo questioned.

"I own the clubs," Damacio reminded his father. "I have to make sure they are being run properly."

"If you say so but remember, if your real work isn't

handled, then you won't be able to own all these clubs you love buying."

"My apologies, father," Damacio said, knowing it was futile trying to have a meaningful conversation with his father about anything he didn't approve of. "What do you need for me to do?"

"I'm meeting with a gentleman who will be buying a significant amount of cocaine and heroin from our organization and I want you there."

"Okay, so when are we meeting with him?"

"Wednesday evening. So, whatever plans you have, cancel them," Alejo stated.

"You said he's buying a significant quantity of drugs, where does he plan to distribute them?"

"Houston and the neighboring states," Alejo said, taking another shot of Rey So Anejo tequila.

"Houston...but that's Allen Collins territory."

"For now, but soon that will change."

"Why? We've been doing business with him for years. Is he no longer happy with our prices or product and going elsewhere?"

"No. I've decided he needs to be replaced and I found someone who will be perfect."

"Father, this is a mistake. Allen Collins and his sons have brought our organization a shit load of money. They have proven how valuable they are."

"Fuck them! Allen thinks he's better than us and Clayton is more arrogant than his father. The only one who shows us respect is Kasir. They need to be humbled!" Alejo spit.

"You're still angry Allen wouldn't let you be a

partner in A. C. Enterprise. You know that was too risky. He explained it to you and you seemed to understand."

"Oh please," Alejo scoffed. "He wanted to be the only respected businessman. On the cover of magazines, and being honored with awards while he turns his nose up at me." Alejo threw up his arms with fury. "How dare he!" Alejo took another shot then slammed his glass down on the table, shattering it.

"Father, calm down." Damacio pleaded. "You're taking this much too personally."

"It is personal! I made him," Alejo pounded his fist. "Allen Collins is rich and powerful because of me. And I will be the reason he loses it all."

"I believe you're making a mistake. You shouldn't underestimate the Collins family. They've proven to be very resourceful," Damacio said.

"Don't you," Alejo yelled pointing his finger at his son, "underestimate me. I'm the head of this organization and if I say we're bringing Allen Collins down, then so be it."

"Okay."

"And I expect you to be at the meeting on Wednesday. Don't disappoint me, Damacio."

"I'll be there, father."

Damacio knew he didn't have a choice unless he wanted to be ostracized from the family like his older brother had been. He figured his father would soften with age but instead he had become more combative and stubborn. Damacio had a feeling there would be severe repercussions for cutting ties with Allen Collins but there was no reasoning with Alejo. Now all Damacio could do is sit back and watch how everything unfolds.

"Yes, I'm on the way," Crystal said as she came out of Starbucks, trying to carry her drink and talk on the phone at the same time. "See you soon." She knew Allen was anal when it came to punctuality but Crystal needed her caffeine fix.

"Crystal!" she heard someone call out her name and turned around.

"Kasir...hi." Her eyes lit up like she was happy to see him but Crystal's voice sounded standoffish.

"I thought that was you but you look so different," Kasir commented, taking a closer look at her attire. The heavy makeup, big hair and cutout bandage dress was replaced with a natural beat, sleek side bun and a lightweight ruffle tie mini skirt and silk blouse.

"Yes, I had a job interview," she said nervously.

"I thought you were in school?" Kasir asked.

"I am but a girl has to get her bills paid."

"I see. I asked Lance to reach out to your friend and give you my number. Did she?"

"Yes, she did. I've been meaning to call you but I've been so hectic with school and trying to find a job."

"Maybe I can help you with that. I have a lot of business relationships with people who do hiring. Do you have a resume?"

"Thank you but that's okay. I have a good feeling

about this interview. I think I'ma get the job," Crystal said, fidgeting with her coffee cup.

"Well good. For some reason if it doesn't work out, don't hesitate to let me know. I'll be more than happy to help you."

"Thank you, Kasir." Crystal gave him a demure smile.

"I was on my way to one of my favorite restaurants down the street to get lunch. Why don't you join me?"

"I would love to but I'm on my way to meet someone and I'm running late. I really do have to go," Crystal said about to rush off.

"Wait!" Kasir grabbed her arm before she could flee. "I apologize. I didn't mean to be so assertive."

"You don't have to apologize."

"Listen, I haven't been able to stop thinking about you since that night we spent together."

"Me neither," Crystal admitted.

'Then come with me," Kasir implored.

"I can't but I promise I'll call you. I promise," Crystal said one more time before hurrying off.

Kasir wanted to chase after her but he held himself back. He knew he needed to let her go. If Crystal wanted to give him a chance, it had to be her decision, not his.

"Now that's the kind of woman I need on my arm," Caesar remarked to his two friends who was sitting with him at the St. Regis hotel in the Tea Lounge.

"Man, I hate to break it to you but she might be way out yo' league," Jeff shook his head.

"This don't happen often but I have to agree with Jeff," Darius shrugged. "That lady don't look like new money. She seems like she been swimming in money for a very long time."

"Your point?" Caesar asked.

"The point is, a woman like that ain't gon' be impressed wit' them fleet of cars you got or taking her on some bullshit shopping spree. My advice to you, I would look but don't approach," Darius chuckled.

"For the moves I'ma 'bout to make, she's exactly the sort of woman I need and luckily I don't take advice from you." Caesar got up from the table to see where the mystery woman had disappeared to. He found her in The Remington Bar. She was sitting on the barstool. Caesar started wondering if maybe she was one of those high-class prostitutes. It was a well-known fact a lot of the upper echelon pussy in Houston would seek out potential clients at the ritzy St. Regis.

"Let me know if I can get you anything else," the bartender said, handing the woman a glass of wine.

"Excuse my bluntness but you are gorgeous. Are you single and what's your name?" Caesar asked.

"My name is Karmen and no I'm not single. Don't you see..." She stopped herself, remembering she had taken off her wedding ring after leaving the private investigators office. Karmen knew her husband was cheating but to see the proof, enraged her. She'd snatched off her ring and almost tossed it out the window but changed her mind. Instead she drove to the St. Regis and decided to have a few drinks to ease her pain.

"Don't I see what?" Caesar stared at Karmen waiting for her to finish her sentence.

"I assumed you saw the ring on my wedding finger but I forgot I took it off."

"I should've known a woman like you was taken. Your husband is a lucky man but I'm sure he knows that."

"Used to think so but not anymore," Karmen sighed, signaling for the bartender to bring her another wine after finishing her first glass.

"Is that the reason you took off your wedding ring?"

"Sure is." Karmen glanced up and for the first time, getting a good look at the handsome man, who was casually dressed in a Givenchy Cuban fit Monkey Brothers graphic t-shirt paired with Givenchy drawstring pants that had a soft wool, slouchy tapered fit. Caesar finished off his leisure look with some Balenciaga high top supple lamb noir leather sneakers that had a metallic shine. Although his attire was laidback, his aura reeked clout.

"When a man doesn't appreciate what he has, then he risks another man stepping in and taking his place."

"I'm sorry, I didn't get your name."

"Caesar."

"Caesar, you seem like a decent guy but even if I wasn't married, you don't look to be any more than twenty-eight or twenty-nine which is much too young for me," Karmen said finishing up her second glass of wine and ready for a third.

"I'm thirty-four and I assumed we were around

the same age, with you being a little younger than me. I guess I was wrong but I don't age discriminate. I like what I like and I like you."

At that moment, Karmen decided to decline a third drink. She knew she was feeling vulnerable and the man standing in front of her was sexy as fuck. He had these full bodied, well-proportioned lips with that bow in the top lip. He even had the cleft chin. Too much wine always made Karmen susceptible to being sexually aroused and as angry as she was with Allen, she had no intentions of cheating on him.

"I really need to be going. It was very nice talking to you," Karmen said abruptly, grabbing her purse.

"Wait." Caesar put his hand on top of hers. "I thought our conversation was going good. Why you rushing off?"

"Yeah, it was going too good," Karmen told him. "I need to get home." She slid her hand from under his and walked off.

"Bye, Mrs. Collins," the bartender called out, waving his hand.

She smiled and waved back at the bartender before exiting out the hotel. Caesar didn't take his eyes off her the entire time.

"You seemed friendly with her. What can you tell me?" Caesar asked, directing his attention to the bartender.

"Not much." But Caesar wasn't convinced. When there was something he wanted, Caesar wasted no time getting it. He placed two bills in front of the bartender, who gladly took them. It was a weekday but business had been much slower than usual.

"So, tell me everything you know about that lovely lady who just walked out of here."

"I don't know a lot but her name is Karmen Collins. Her husband is Allen Collins. They come here sometimes but usually they sit in the restaurant area for dinner."

"What does her husband do?"

"Some bigwig businessman. I've seen him on the news a few times being interviewed. He seems to have it all...money, prestige, and of course a beautiful wife," the bartender smiled. "She's gorgeous and surprisingly very sweet. Mrs. Collins is one of my best tippers," he nodded. "Other than that, they seem like any other happily married rich couple."

Caesar took in what the bartender told him. He was pretty sure everything he said was true except for the happily married part. He wanted to find out all he could about Allen Collins, especially since he planned on taking his wife away from him.

Chapter Eleven

Have No Fear

"Back so soon from your trip," Clayton said when he walked in the kitchen and saw Ashton getting a protein drink from the refrigerator.

"I've been home for a couple days now and I would give anything to get back on a plane to Miami."

"What's stopping you?"

"Something called school." Ashton rolled her eyes. "Luckily I only have one year left."

"Why even do the year? We both know you're not going to do anything with the degree you receive," Clayton cracked.

"Why are you here? You have your own place," Ashton scoffed, slamming the refrigerator as Clayton was reaching inside to get his own drink.

"Don't get yourself worked up and break a nail because I'm speaking the truth. You have no interest in school. That's not a secret."

"It's also not a secret if I don't go to school, my allowance gets cut off. A girl has to live."

"You could always do something like get a job," Clayton mocked. "I know that word is a bit foreign to you since most people don't consider club hopping to be real work."

"Big brother you prove even if a person wears a designer suit, they can still be trash. As long as our father cuts the checks which includes yours, don't worry about my job skills."

"You should consider being a little nicer. Dad might not always be the one cutting your checks."

Ashton eyed Clayton strangely, ready to ask him what in the hell did he mean by that. But she saw Damacio calling and she was much more interested in speaking to him than her pompous brother.

"Hey!" Ashton answered in a sweet voice, walking out the kitchen with a dreamy look on her face. The sudden change in demeanor didn't go unnoticed by Clayton.

"Who in the world has you grinning so hard," he mumbled. Following his curiosity, Clayton walked out the kitchen to see if he could find out who his sister was talking to. He had never seen her act so giddy over anyone except for their father, and it was when he bought her a brand new Benz for her birthday or the time he took her on an unlimited spending shopping spree when she graduated from high school.

"You've only been gone for a couple days and I'm ready for you to come back," Damacio told her.

"I know what you mean. I was just telling my brother I was ready to get on a plane back to Miami."

"Then come."

"You know I have school. My mother would kill me if I cut classes to go have more fun in Miami."

"I guess that means I'm to coming to you," Damacio said.

"Are you serious? You're coming to Houston… when?"

"I have a meeting my father needs me to be at, tonight, so I can be there either Thursday or Friday night."

"Don't play with me. Are you really coming?" Ashton didn't want to get excited until she was positive she would see Damacio.

"I promise I'm coming. I need to see you. My bed hasn't felt the same since you haven't been in it."

"And nobody else better be in it either."

"That goes both ways. You're mine now. I'll see you soon."

"See you soon. Bye, babe." Ashton blew him a kiss.

"Bye."

"Well…well…well, does my little sister have a boyfriend?"

Ashton jumped when she heard Clayton's voice. "Were you ear hustling on my conversation?" she barked.

"I was simply walking by and heard you sounding like a lovesick puppy."

"Shut up, Clayton! And stay out of my business!" Ashton yelled running upstairs.

Now you know I can't mind my business, Clayton thought, laughing to himself.

"Dad, have we gotten our new shipment in?" Kasir needed to know. "I've received several phone calls from our buyers wanting to re-up on product and we have nothing to give."

"Are you saying we still haven't gotten our product? Are you sure?" Allen put down the files he was going over to give his son his full attention.

"I called the warehouse and spoke to TJ before I came to see you. He said we haven't received anything."

"Did you call Alejo or Damacio to find out what the fuckin' hold up is? That shipment was supposed to be here over a week ago."

"I didn't want to call them until I spoke to you."

"Get them on the phone now! I had no idea we never received our product."

"Dad, I mentioned it to you last week. You told me not to worry, it would be here any day," Kasir reminded his father while calling Alejo.

"I don't remember, maybe you did but this shit needs to be handled," Allen fumed.

"Alejo didn't answer, let me try Damacio...he's not

answering either," Kasir huffed.

"What in the hell is going on," Allen said shaking his head.

"You know that's one of the biggest orders we've placed. It was so large, Alejo asked us to pay upfront. Which you signed off on."

"I know!" Allen shifted in his chair tossing down his pen. "After all that bullshit went down with his nephews, I wanted Alejo to know all was forgiven and we were moving forward. We've never had any problems receiving our product on time, normally it comes early. I'm sure there's a reasonable explanation."

"Hope you're right," Kasir said but he had a bad feeling.

"You just keep calling until you get one of them on the phone or we'll be on the next flight to Miami," Allen stated without hesitation.

"Alejo Hernandez, it's a pleasure to meet you in person instead of just speaking with you over the phone."

"The pleasure is all mine," Alejo said shaking his hand. "I'm glad you were able to come a little early. I wanted to speak with you before my son arrives. When I heard about your Houston ambitions in the drug market, I felt we could form a beautiful and mutually beneficial relationship."

"I'll admit, I was surprised when I heard you were trying to connect with me but intrigued with the idea of us doing business together."

"I pride myself on being...what do you Americans say, ahead of the curve," Alejo chuckled loudly. "And you, Caesar, I believe has what it takes to dominate the drug market and I want to help you do that."

"I see," Caesar said leaning back in his chair. "One of the reasons I was surprised you reached out to me, is because when I made the decision to relocate to Houston, I did some research."

"Of course, like any good business man would."

"Yes. When I was deciding who I could get the best prices from for the high volume I planned to move, you were someone I considered brokering a deal with. But several of my sources told me you had a person already in place for the Houston market."

"Your sources were correct," Alejo acknowledged.

"If it's true, wouldn't that be a conflict of interest? I mean, the drug market is huge but it ain't big enough for there to be two kings."

"Ha!" Alejo slapped his leg and once again laughed loudly. "I knew I would like you, Caesar. You are absolutely right," he nodded. "That's why from here on out, I will only be supplying to you. You will be the only king," Alejo winked.

"Now you're talking my language," Caesar winked back. "Might I ask, why you will no longer be supplying drugs to the person you were dealing with before?"

"Yes, you may. The relationship is no longer mutually beneficial. When I first started doing business with Allen Collins, he was hungry for money and power. Then he used his drug earnings to make him some big man

around town. The CEO of a multimillion dollar legal corporation...please," Alejo scoffed. "That company is run
off drug money. But I'll get the last laugh." Alejo's eyes
were piercing with anger. "In Allen's quest to achieve
power in the corporate world, he lost his hunger. Without hunger, I no longer benefit in our partnership, so it
was time for me to sever our relationship."

"It sounds personal."

Alejo leaned forward as if about to tell a deep dark
secret. "When you're making this type of money, it's
always personal."

This meeting was turning out to be more informa-
tive than Caesar had ever imagined. Houston was a big
city but it wasn't big enough for there to be two men
with the name Allen Collins both making major moves.
Which meant the Allen Collins that Alejo had been
speaking of had to be the man married to the woman
he'd become instantly enamored with, Karmen. Caesar
never pegged her for the wife of a drug kingpin. But he
also knew he was correct with his assessment of her.
The level of success Allen Collins had reached required
a certain caliber of woman by his side and Karmen was
it. What Caesar learned tonight, only solidified that.

"Damacio, there you are and right on time," Alejo
grinned after glancing at his watch. "I want you to meet
our newest partner. Caesar, this is my son, Damacio."

"It's good to meet you." Caesar stood up and shook
Damacio's hand.

"Likewise. My father told me you were interested
in taking over the Houston market. Where were you
doing business before?" Damacio asked.

"New York. I did very well there but it was time to move on, if you know what I mean."

"I do," Alejo agreed. "It's never good to overstay your welcome."

"I'm sure you have family there. Will they be relocating with you?"

"I hope my son's questions don't seem too intrusive," Alejo said. "He always believes it's important to know who we're doing business with, especially if it's long-term."

"I totally understand. You've been so open with me, Alejo, and you deserve the same from me. My family won't be relocating with me, at least not right now. New York is their home and my home is now Houston. It's the place I plan to build my empire."

"And we will do everything we can to make that possible. Isn't that right, Damacio?"

"Of course, father."

"Great! Now we eat. My chef has prepared an amazing dinner for us. Follow me to the dining room," Alejo said, leading the way.

Caesar and Alejo were being extra chummy as they walked to the dining room while Damacio observed in silence. He hadn't yet sized Caesar up. Damacio's first impression was a man with an easy-going persona, who would have no problem fitting in, in just about any environment. He came across as very non-threatening. Off the cuff, that trait would put most at ease but it was the opposite for Damacio. Caesar's laidback demeanor gave him reason to pause. Most people would feel somewhat intimidated breaking bread with a man like

Alejo Hernandez. His reputation was notorious in the drug trafficking world yet Caesar didn't flinch. If he was nervous or afraid, he covered it up like a chameleon. On the flip side, if Caesar wasn't worried, it meant dealing with someone on Alejo's level was nothing new to him. If that was the case, it concerned Damacio even more. A man with no fear, is a man to fear.

Chapter Twelve

Your Secret Is Safe With Me

"You still haven't heard anything from Alejo or Damacio," Clayton stated dumbfounded.

"I'm praying this situation isn't as bad as I think it is," Kasir said, as stress weighed in on him.

"It's worse. I can't believe our father wasn't on top of this sooner," Clayton shook his head setting the stage for the let's blame dad game. "Normally, he's trying to get tracking information on products before they even had a chance to ship. We're almost two weeks in before he decides to make a move. Nah, that shit don't make sense. I told you he was slipping."

"You might be right. Before it got this far, I mentioned to dad the shipment was late but he basically brushed me off. He forgot I even asked him about it and he never followed up."

"I'm glad you're both here," Allen said coming into Kasir's office unexpectedly, surprising both brothers. They glanced at each other, hoping their father hadn't overheard their conversation.

"Dad, I was about to call you," Kasir said nervously.

"Well now you don't have to call me because I'm here. I'm assuming you still haven't made contact with anyone in the Hernandez family."

"No, I haven't."

"Neither have I so I'm heading to Miami tonight," Allen told his sons.

"I can come with you," Clayton offered.

"No, you stay here. I want Kasir to come. Alejo seems to like him, even has a certain level of respect."

"Not enough respect to answer or return any of his phone calls," Clayton countered. His father shot him a look that was nothing pleasant.

"Even so, I believe bringing Kasir with me will be more beneficial than bringing you. Alejo felt disrespected by you at our last meeting if you recall," Allen huffed.

"You mean for bringing proof that his nephews were some fuckin' thieves? Not only were they screwing us, they were screwing him too. If anything, the cocky motherfucker should be thanking me," Clayton barked.

"And that's why you're staying here. I don't need your hot-headed ass coming, no matter how right you might be," Allen told his youngest son before turning his attention back to Kasir. "The private jet leaves at seven so be ready."

"Dad, I really think you should bring me too. We need to show a united front," Clayton insisted.

"Listen, this trip is to find out what the hell is going on with Alejo and whatever it is, get the situation resolved. The bottom line we need our product and we're going to Miami to get it," Allen rationalized.

"Have you thought about what we're going to do if we don't get it?" Kasir questioned.

Both Allen and Clayton turned to Kasir with a raised eyebrow. He was normally the optimistic one. Believing all could be worked out in business, if both sides sat down and had a meaningful conversation. But there wasn't a trace of optimism being heard from Kasir today.

"Yeah, dad, what are we going to do when Alejo shoots you down?" Clayton chimed in.

"That won't happen. I've known Alejo since before the two of you were even born. Our history runs deep. Alejo has a lot of pride and sometimes it can cause him to overreact. Instead of continuing to call him, if I come to his home in Miami, he will feel I'm showing him respect."

"The shit load of money you dropped for the last shipment, should've showed that man all the respect he needs," Clayton scoffed.

"Son, let me handle this. I know what the fuck I'm

doing," Allen snapped. "Kasir, I'll see you on the plane. Don't be late," was Allen's departing words, slamming the door on his way out.

"Damn, Clayton, you just had to say some shit you knew would get under his skin," Kasir shook his head in dismay.

"All I did was speak the truth. I've been telling ya' that crazy sonofabitch Alejo couldn't be trusted. And dad's stubborn ass doesn't want to admit I was right."

"Real talk, I'm hoping you're wrong. Because if you are right, shit is about to get ugly," Kasir predicted.

Crystal had been sitting on top of her bed for the last hour debating if she should text Kasir or not. He'd consumed her thoughts since the night they had what she considered, mind-blowing sex. It only got worse when she ran into him coming out of Starbucks.

If my life wasn't so fuckin' complicated I would've been called him. But what if he finds out I'm dating a married man, which would eventually happen. After so many times of me denying him access to my crib, he will no doubt become suspicious. He'll probably think I live with my boyfriend, Crystal sighed while continuing to figure shit out in her head. *Why do I have to like him so much! My life was going just fine until I met Kasir. Being with him will only bring more craziness to my life but he is so worth it*, Crystal decided.

Hey, it's me, Crystal. I can't get you off my mind. How are you?

Crystal felt this nervousness in the pit of her stomach. It was a throwback to the teenage love type feelings. She threw her phone down on the bed, becoming scared he wouldn't respond because she waited too long to reach out.

"Gosh, I hope I didn't fuck this up!" Crystal screamed, picking her phone back up to see if he'd hit her back. After fifteen minutes and no reply, she was ready to rip her hair out. "I hate him!" she yelled, storming out her room to the kitchen.

"If this nigga ain't replied by the time I get back to my bedroom, I might break my fuckin' phone," Crystal seethed putting a bag of kettle corn in the microwave. She hoped the sweet and salty taste of her favorite treat would lessen the blow of feeling rejected. To further help her cause, Crystal poured a glass of champagne, filling it all the way to the top. Instead of putting the bottle back in the refrigerator, she carried it to the bedroom with her. The first thing she did upon entering was grab her phone and once again, disappointment ensued.

"Maybe I should call him," she said out loud, reaching for her phone again but then dropping it. "Nah, I might come across as overly pressed," she sighed. Then it happened. Her smile became so wide you could've put a foot in it.

Kasir: You've been on my mind too.
I want to see you.

Crystal: I want to see you too.
How about tonight?

Kasir: Would love that but I
have to go out of town.
Will be back tomorrow.

Crystal: :(

Kasir: Don't be sad. How about
I take you out for dinner
when I get back?

Crystal: That would turn my
frown into a smile.

Kasir: Perfect. I'll call you
when I get back.

Crystal: I'll be waiting.

"I think I'm in lust!" Crystal gushed, flopping down on the bed holding on to her phone. She still had that starry eyed glaze on her face and it wasn't going away anytime soon.

"Clayton, I'm surprised to see you here," Karmen said kissing her son on the cheek. "I thought you would be on the company jet with your father and Kasir.

"Dad didn't want me to go. He felt I would ruin the meeting. So, he took his favorite son and left me here."

"Clayton, your father loves you and Kasir equally." She stroked the side of her son's face, seeing how upset he was. "Come sit down." She led Clayton over to the chair near the piano.

"Mother, you know I'm right. No matter how hard I try or what deals I bring to the table, Kasir always comes off as the golden boy."

"Have a drink and relax while I play one of your favorites." Karmen sat down at the piano and her long slender fingers began gliding over each note to Moonlight Sonata by Beethoven. Ever since Clayton was a little boy, whenever his mother played this song on the piano, it would calm his soul as if magic was sprinkled in the air.

Clayton watched as his mother closed her eyes and played the classical yet romantic piece with her typical grace. No matter how many times he heard her play it, Clayton was always moved. She had him in a trance until the very last note.

"Bravo!" he clapped.

"Thank you." Karmen smiled.

"You seemed to be playing with even more passion than usual. As if this wasn't just about making me feel better, you wanted to feel better too," Clayton said.

"You've always been so observant. Much too wise for you age." Karmen let out a deep sigh.

"Mother, is something wrong? If so you can tell me." Clayton sat down next to his mother at the piano and took her hand.

"Your father is having an affair," Karmen stated being completely transparent with her son.

"Are you sure?"

"Positive. He's been seeing some woman named Crystal. I first saw her at the gala where your father was being honored. I became suspicious and hired a private investigator. He has her living at one of the corporate apartments."

"Mother, I'm so sorry." Clayton leaned in and hugged her. "Father doesn't deserve you, he never has. What are you going to do?"

"I'm not sure. I still love your father very much and our family means everything to me. Until I decide what I want to do, please don't mention this to your father, Kasir, or Ashton. Promise me, Clayton."

"I promise. Your secret is safe with me. I won't utter a word."

"Thank you," she said squeezing Clayton's hand tightly. "Ashton is going to be home late. Why don't you come have dinner with me, it'll be just the two of us."

"I would love that, mother."

Having Clayton there with her and telling him the truth actually brought Karmen a sense of comfort. He was no longer a child she had to shield and protect, he was a grown man she could trust. Not only was he her son, he had now become a confidant.

Chapter Thirteen

Bad Business

"How much longer do you think Alejo is going to keep us waiting?" Kasir whispered to his father.

"I don't fuckin' know. Clearly, he's trying to make a point," Allen mumbled through clenched teeth. "But we're here now and we ain't leaving until we speak to him."

"Maybe we..."

"Please forgive me," Alejo came into the living room apologizing profusely before Kasir could finish his sentence.

"No need to apologize. We're family," Allen stood up and said as the two men hugged.

"Kasir, always good to see you." Alejo shook his hand and smiled. "Where is Clayton?"

"He couldn't make it but he wanted me to tell you hello. Is Damacio here?"

"No, my son went out of town. Probably off trying to open another nightclub," Alejo laughed. "I'm sure a busy man like you didn't come all the way to Miami to talk about Damacio. What can I do for you, Allen?"

Kasir and Allen gave each other a quick glance. It struck them as odd, Alejo was acting as if he wasn't holding their fuckin' shipment hostage. They weren't sure what kind of game he was playing but they planned to end it now.

"Alejo, I'm sure you're aware we haven't received a huge shipment which we paid for in advance," Allen stated.

"Oh, that," Alejo said before standing up and pouring himself a glass of tequila. "Allen, we've been doing business for many, many years."

"Yes, we have. That's why I'm surprised our shipment is so late. Both myself and Kasir have been calling you and Damacio for over a week now. Neither of you have responded. Is there some sort of delay in the shipment? I know things come up unexpectedly. Is there a problem?" Allen questioned.

"Allen, you must be proud of yourself. You are the epitome of a calm, in control business mogul. I know you want to put a knife through my heart, instead you stand there like you're in a room full of Fortune 500

CEO's. I'm impressed." Alejo began clapping his hands together insultingly.

"What is your fuckin' problem, Alejo! Spit the shit out and stop wasting my motherfuckin' time," Allen demanded.

"Aha, now that's the Allen I know." Alejo grinned widely. "You thought coming here to my home and leaving Clayton back in Houston would impress me. Humph, I would've been more impressed if you'd brought your cocky son along. At least I would know you still had some balls," he scoffed, shaking his head.

"Father, don't." Kasir held his dad's arm as he seemed ready to charge at Alejo like a raging bull.

"No, no, let him go. Let's see if Allen has any fight left in him," Alejo laughed, taunting his opponent.

"I think we all need to relax, so we can sit down and have a reasonable discussion," Kasir proposed.

"My dear, Kasir, always being the voice of reason. I guess that's why your father brought you. You're so transparent, Allen. I thought after all these years, you would've learned some new tricks. But no, I guess you're just an old dog now," Alejo chuckled.

"So, let me keep a clear understanding. You think you're going to take my money and keep my drugs?"

"That's exactly what I'm going to do, Allen, and there isn't a damn thing you can do about it," Alejo growled. "You can't run and report me to the police or call one of your big shot friends you play golf with. Then they would know you're a common crook just like me."

"Now I get it." Allen walked up on Alejo and stared down at him. Alejo was much shorter than the six-two

Allen but his ruthless tactics made him a giant.

"Get what?"

"Jealousy. You vindictive old man. No wonder you live in this big ass house all alone, except for your hired help. Your heart is full of jealousy. You want to end our profitable relationship because you're jealous that I did what you couldn't...run a legitimate, successful business. Well, get the fuck over it!" Allen scolded.

"Legitimate! Your business is run on drug money. See how long you stay on top without it," Alejo warned. Then, without warning, Allen grabbed Alejo by the throat and lifted him off the floor, with one hand. He was almost fifty but strong and built like a man half his age.

"Dad!" Kasir yelled watching the color drain from Alejo's face. Less than thirty seconds later Gilberto and two other men stormed in the room with guns drawn.

"Put Senor Hernandez down now!" Gilberto ordered, aiming his weapon directly at Allen.

Allen delayed following the command, even with a gun aimed at his head. Seeing the life leave Alejo's eyes was bringing him too much satisfaction.

"Father, let him go!" Kasir stood in front of his dad and belted. Allen was breathing heavy and he seemed to be in a trance but reality kicked in and he didn't want to die, right there in front of his son, so he let Alejo go.

His men came running towards Alejo, who was laid out on the floor, trying desperately to catch his breath. One of his workers retrieved a bottle of water as Alejo continued to struggle.

"This didn't turn out well," Kasir mouthed to his

father who looked like he was ready to attack Alejo again.

"You get out of my home now and don't come back or you're a dead man," Alejo threatened between harsh coughs.

"Come on, let's go," Kasir said, leading his father out before things erupted again.

Father and son remained silent until they reached their awaiting car. "Back to the airport," Allen told the driver.

"What just happened in there," Kasir sighed. "I'm surprised Alejo didn't just kill us right then. We were checked before we came in, so he knew we weren't carrying."

"Please, that sonofabitch wants to see me suffer. If Alejo killed me now, it would take away all the fun," Allen huffed. "But if he thinks I'ma let this go, he's underestimating me."

"Dad, we do have to be careful. Several business ventures are coming up, including Lance's Reps Up International deal. We don't need any negative press."

"All the shit you just said is what Alejo is counting on." Allen seethed. "We have to make a move and fast."

"What do you have in mind?"

"First thing is, we have to find a new supplier."

"I have some possible leads," Kasir said.

"The quality has to be on point. Our customers have already been waiting long enough. Soon they'll go elsewhere."

"We have a loyal clientele."

"Kasir," Allen paused staring at his son, making

sure he had his full attention. "When it comes to stopping someone from making money, their loyalty ends. Trust me, our so called loyal clientele will be looking elsewhere for their product."

"Dad, I'm on it."

"We'll have to use money from my personal account on the new order. Fuck!" Allen barked.

"That's a lot of cash to withdraw from your personal account, dad."

"We don't have a choice. I used all of our untraceable cash for the last order with Alejo." The more Allen thought about the predicament he was in the more incensed he became.

Allen was the CEO of a multimillion dollar conglomerate but part of having a legitimate business meant most of his corporate funds were tied up and there was no way he was going to liquidate assets. In the past, that had never been a problem because his lucrative drug business provided an endless cash flow. Having both entities was equivalent to the perfect marriage. Alejo had singlehandedly destroyed that union and Allen planned to make him pay dearly.

"You have the softest skin," Damacio looked up and said while sprinkling soft kisses on the inside of Ashton's thighs. Each kiss led further up until his tongue licked her wet clit.

Ashton bit down on her lip and started to pull

away but Damacio latched on to her wrist pinning her down. He didn't want her to escape. He wanted Ashton's body to surrender to all the pleasure he was giving her. Once Damacio slid inside, Ashton could no longer hold back her cries of pleasure.

"You love driving me crazy," she purred breathlessly.

"I do," Damacio said biting down on her neck which only made Ashton more aroused. He had a way of mixing sensual strokes of pleasure with dabs of gratifying pain that continuously blew Ashton's mind.

"I'm gonna start calling you my hot, Latin lover," Ashton turned and said to Damacio after they finished making love.

Damacio leaned over and kissed Ashton softly on her full lips. He then grabbed her at the nape of her hair and whispered in her ear. "You better call me more than just that."

"Baby, I was only joking. You know you're more than just a lover to me, although you are super hot," Ashton smiled.

"And you're super sexy." Damacio buried his nose in Ashton's hair, taking in her scent that always lured him in.

Damacio and Ashton had what you could describe as the dopamine effect and they had it bad for each other. So bad that what most would consider scorching lust, the two of them considered being in deep love.

"So sexy that you only have eyes for me?" Ashton questioned.

"Every woman who passes my eyes, I only see you.

I wanna wake up and go to sleep next to you, every day and every night."

"I feel the same way," Ashton said, kissing on Damacio once again.

"Good, because I've decided to get a place in Houston and I want you to live with me," Damacio told her.

"Are you serious...you're leaving Miami? But what about your clubs?"

"Do you want me here or not?"

"Of course, I want you here. How can you even ask me that?" Ashton moved closer to Damacio, making sure her naked body was touching his.

"My clubs in Miami will be fine. I have someone who can oversee them. I've already started looking for locations here in Houston."

"You're going to open a club here! That's going to be amazing."

"Yes, it is and I want you to be right by my side."

"I better be." Ashton nuzzled the tip of her nose underneath Damacio's chin. "So, when are you moving here? Having you inside of me for the last couple days already has me spoiled. I need this dick like every day. You got me addicted."

"I know, it was my plan all along. Just like the night I brought Shanice to the club with me."

"What!?" Ashton lifted her body up in the bed and stared at Damacio. "What do you mean like you brought Shanice?"

"You were trying to play so hard to get but I knew if you saw me with another woman, your competitive/ jealous nature would kick in," he laughed.

"You didn't even know I was going to be at the club that night!" Ashton folded her arms still not believing Damacio had somewhat orchestrated her feelings of resentment upon seeing him with another woman.

"I kept at least one of my men on you from the moment you were dropped off at your hotel," Damacio revealed.

"Why did you do that?" she gave him a puzzled look.

"Because I wanted you and I refused to take no for an answer. I also knew you wanted me too but was trying to fight it. I simply gave you the motivation you needed to give in to temptation."

"I can't believe you played with my emotions like that!" Ashton popped, smacking Damacio on his shoulder. "But I'm glad you did," she blushed.

"I knew you would be."

"You're so damn cocky...but I love it. But you still haven't answered my question. When are you moving here?"

"Let's start looking tomorrow. How big do you want the house to be?"

"I've lived in big houses all my life. I want us to live in a super sexy penthouse, because we're super sexy," she teased.

"Penthouse it is. We have an appointment with the realtor at noon."

"You already have a realtor? How did you...never mind," Ashton shrugged. There was no need for her to ask Damacio how he knew she would be excited about him moving to Houston and agreeing to live with him.

They were completely hooked on one another and Damacio was positive of that, even before Ashton was willing to admit it. So, instead of wasting anymore time discussing their obsession for each other, they spent the duration of the night making passionate love over and over again.

Chapter Fourteen

We Meet Again

"My niggas! Is you ready for this! We 'bout to take over Houston!" Caesar announced in the middle of the top floor hotel suite, in front of a room full of people.

"Man, we been ready!" Darius boasted. "You know how we do. These down south mutherfuckas ain't ready for us New Yorkers." The room exploded with laughter.

"They better get ready, 'cause we takin' over," Jeff winked.

"Yes, we are," Caesar nodded. Raising the magnum bottle of champagne he was holding up high. Caesar felt like he was having his *New Jack City*, Nino Brown moment. His entire crew from NYC was there with him celebrating. They had big plans and tonight was only the beginning.

"Yo this shit really comin' together," Darius said to Caesar as they walked outside on the balcony to talk.

"I know. I didn't think it would happen this fast but I'm damn sure happy it has. Linking up wit' Alejo was a game changer."

"For sure. That worked out lovely. Six months ago, the pressure was on and we were scrambling to get the fuck outta New York, not sure how things would unfold. Now here we are, literally on top," Darius stated as the men gazed at the city views.

"Yep. We 'bout to be the dominate drug ring in Houston and the surrounding areas. Ain't nobody gon' fuck wit' us. We got prime product but most importantly, our entire team is on deck," Caesar said proudly, glancing back watching them drinking, smoking, laughing, and just enjoying themselves.

"This is what it's all about. Us being together, making it do what it do," Darius smiled.

"Baby, when you coming back inside? I don't wanna be sittin' in there without you," Brianna said walking up behind Caesar and placing her arms around his waist.

"I'm talkin' to Darius. I'll be back in there shortly," he assured her.

"Good. I don't like being alone." Briana leaned forward and lifted her head up, kissing Caesar before going back inside.

"I'm sure Brianna is thrilled you changed your mind and decided to bring her to Houston instead of leaving her in New York," Darius commented when she walked off.

"Yeah, but I'm regretting that shit already," Caesar shook his head. "She so fuckin' clingy."

"Man, it's yo' own fuckin' fault. That's what you get for spoiling her ass. Money ain't enough to keep Briana happy, she wants yo' time too," Darius joked.

"You laughing but you know you tellin' the truth. I'm not used to sleeping alone and besides the married chick I met at the hotel, ain't nobody caught my eye. It was either bring Brianna down here or beat my shit. At the time, she seemed like the best option but now not so much," Caesar shrugged. "I should've waited."

"Waited...why you met someone that quick?"

"Nah, I just think my first option might become a real possibility."

"Not the married chick?!" Darius frowned up his face. "Man, that chick is way out yo' league. No disrespect but this the no lie zone over here. Plus, you said she's married."

"First off, I'm 'bout to run Houston. I only want a top notch lady to represent me."

"Yeah, you 'bout to run the streets. You already said her man some corporate giant. She not used to dealing wit' drug dealers."

"I assumed the same thing but being a CEO in the corporate world is actually her husband's side hustle."

"I'm not following you?" Darius raised an eyebrow.

"That nigga is the real kingpin out this mutherfucka!" Caesar laughed. "Well he was until Alejo cut him off and started selling all his product to me."

"Wait, that nigga was moving product for yo' new connect?" Darius wanted confirmation.

"Sure was. I'm talkin' major supply. Corporate nigga by day, drug kingpin by night. So that bad bitch he's married to is just the type of woman I need to be my queen."

"I would've never thought," Darius shook his head. "That man has managed to do what most call the fuckin' impossible in this drug game. He made his white-collar visions and ambitions a reality. I salute that nigga," he nodded with respect.

"I would salute him too if I didn't want his woman."

"We always want what we can't have. Leave that woman alone. She's married."

"Not happily married," Caesar countered.

"You figured that out from a twenty-minute conversation?"

"Yep. And now that I know she 'bout that life, I want her by my side. I'll treat her right too. Not take her for granted like her husband did."

"Wow. Let me find out you sprung and ain't even got the pussy," Darius cracked.

"Man, we gettin' older. I ain't twenty-one no more. I done ran through so much pussy. Blew so much fuckin' money and my black ass done came close to doing double digits in the federal lockup one too many times. I have to stop gambling wit' my life and focus on the ultimate prize. A woman like Karmen would help me get there." Caesar glanced over his shoulder. "Chicks like Brianna are fun to play wit' but I'm tired of playing."

"I hear you but be careful. A man will kill you over his wife, especially one like the lady you fixated on," Darius warned.

"Trust me, I got this. If things went down the way Alejo made it seem, Allen Collins will be too preoccupied trying to get his business in order. By the time he realizes his marriage is in trouble, Karmen will be gone and his wife will be calling me her man," Caesar stated confidently.

"Good morning," Allen said kissing his wife on her lips. "You were already sleep when I got in last night."

"That's been happening a lot lately," Karmen replied coyly.

"I apologize. With everything going on at the office and then dealing with Alejo, my time has been limited."

"I understand. Do you think you and Alejo will be able to work things out?"

"No. He hasn't reached out since Kasir and I went to see him. You know how stubborn he can be."

"Do you want me to call him?" Karmen asked.

"No but thank you for offering." Allen kissed his wife again. "Alejo has always had a soft spot for you. He might see this as an opportunity to finally take you away from me," Allen joked. "But I know that would never happen."

"Of course, but I really don't mind speaking to him. You haven't been yourself the last few weeks. I can tell this situation is stressing you out. I want to help if I can," Karmen told her husband.

"You're such an amazing woman and wife. I can't imagine my life without you," Allen stroked Karmen's cheek. "Don't worry. I'll handle Alejo and this too shall pass. When it does, we'll go on that vacation I've been promising to take you on for the last few months."

Karmen smiled demurely as Allen left to start his day. In the past, she never worried about where her husband was going because she always assumed wherever it was, it was to better their family. Now, not so much. He could be making a stop to the condo, he had his mistress stashed at for a quick fuck. Those were the type of thoughts that now consumed Karmen's mind.

"I can't stay in this house all day, driving myself crazy with this bullshit," Karmen mumbled out loud, going into the master bathroom. She turned the knob and got in the shower. Karmen decided to do something she hadn't done in a very long time...go on a shopping spree. Normally, she utilized her personal shopper and rarely stepped foot in a store but today was different. She welcomed the chaos of going to the mall and having to interact with strangers. Anything to take her mind off of wondering all day if her husband was being sexually pleasured by another woman.

"Mrs. Collins, we appreciate your business. Please come back anytime. Here's my card," the extra bubbly sales manager smiled. She had every reason to be enthusiastic. Karmen splurged a pretty penny in the Louis Vuitton store and the manager welcomed her return.

"Thank you. You were very helpful," Karmen said, taking her bags and heading out.

"Damn, did you see the rock on her finger!" Brianna whispered loudly to Caesar as they were coming into the Louis Vuitton store and Karmen was exiting out. "When you gon' get me a ring like that? Now that you've moved me to Houston. Don't you think it's time you wife me up," she popped, tossing her hair over her shoulder.

"Here." Caesar handed Brianna a large stack of money. "I forgot something in the car. I'll be right back," he told her.

"Okay! Take your time." Brianna's eyes lit up thinking about how she was about to spend every last dollar Caesar handed her while stuffing the money in her purse.

Caesar was already out the store before Brianna finished talking. He wanted to catch up with Karmen before she went missing. After going back to the hotel, he first saw her at, a few times with no luck, Caesar didn't want to take the chance that he would never run into Karmen again. With the two extra-large Louis Vuitton bags she was carrying, Caesar easily spotted her headed towards the elevators.

"Let me help you with your bags," Caesar said, walking next to Karmen.

"No, thank you," she replied before looking over and doing a double take. "Do I know you?"

"Caesar. I met you a couple weeks ago at the St. Regis."

"That's right. You were sitting at the bar next to me."

"You sure you don't need help with your bags?" he offered again after Karmen seemed to be struggling.

"Sure." Caesar gladly took both bags out of Karmen's hands and she hit the button as they waited for the doors to open.

"I see you put your wedding ring back on. I guess things are better between you and your husband," Caesar commented after they stepped onto the elevator.

Karmen glanced down at her hand and fidgeted with the enormous diamond that was hard to miss. "I'm actually headed to my car to drop off my bags so I can do some more shopping. I'm sure you don't feel like walking me all the way out," Karmen said trying to sidestep questions regarding her marriage.

"I don't mind," Caesar said unable to stop staring at Karmen. "You really are a beautiful woman."

"Thank you." Karmen could feel herself blushing which made her uncomfortable.

"I'll never understand how your husband could take a woman like you for granted."

"This conversation is completely inappropriate," Karmen said sternly, repeatedly pressing down on one of the elevator buttons, as if it would miraculously make it go faster. "I was dealing with some issues when we first met and I was wrong to share that with you."

"No, you weren't. Sometimes we need to vent our frustrations."

"I'm committed to my marriage and my husband." Karmen felt the need to let Caesar know.

"But is he committed to you?" Caesar's question felt like a sharp jab in Karmen's heart. She wasn't sure if he even realized how close he was hitting to home.

"That is none of your business!" she snapped.

"I guess that means no."

"Are you enjoying making a mockery of my marriage?"

"Karmen, that's not what I'm trying to do."

"Really, then what do you call it?"

"Trying to convince you to give me an opportunity to show you I'm the better man for you," Caesar stated. "I'll admit, I might be going about it the wrong way."

Karmen was relieved when the elevator doors opened. She quickly got off, wanting to get away from Caesar but it was for all the wrong reasons. She hated herself for being attracted to this man that she barely even knew. Shame flooded her.

"I'll take these," Karmen said tersely. She then struggled to get the bags out of Caesar's hands.

"Relax. This is the second time you've tried to run away from me."

"Give me my bags. I need to go home."

"I thought we were dropping these off so you could continue shopping?"

"I just remembered I have something I need to take care of." Karmen was visibly flustered.

"Then let me at least walk you to your car."

"No! I don't need your help." Karmen again tried to grab her bags away from Caesar but he was holding onto them tightly. Her hands were now resting on top of his and they both stood in the middle of the busy mall staring at each other.

Karmen had never been drawn to any other man since the day she met Allen over twenty years ago. He was the first and only man she'd ever been intimate with and up until this very moment, she believed he would be the last.

"You don't have to be afraid. You can stop fighting it." Caesar sounded like he was giving Karmen permission to give into temptation but she was resolute to remain strong. Her attraction to him was undeniable. One of the reasons was because Caesar's persistence was reminiscent of how Allen pursued her all those years ago. Karmen loved his confidence and his refusal to be dissuaded.

"I want you to hand me my bags so I can walk out this mall...please."

Caesar reluctantly obliged Karmen's request. Knowing she wouldn't put it in her phone, he asked a woman who was walking by for a pen. He quickly wrote down his phone number on the back of some business card that was in his pocket.

"When your husband disappoints you again, call me. I'll be there for you." Caesar handed Karmen the card. Instead of tossing it in the trash like she knew she should've done, Karmen put the card in her wallet for safe keeping.

Chapter Fifteen

Cheers

"We received our new product last night," Kasir told his father and Clayton while sitting down for a morning meeting.

"How's the quality?" Allen questioned.

"I can't lie. It's not as good as Alejo's but we got an excellent price and it's good enough to hold us over until we find a better plug," Kasir stated.

"We figured that but this will do for now," Allen nodded. "Most important is we have product in stock. Start moving it immediately. The streets have been dry for too long."

"Already started. Two of our major buyers came through late last night," Kasir informed his father.

"Great!" Allen smiled.

"Don't get happy just yet," Clayton jumped in and said.

Allen and Kasir turned to Clayton. Out of the three of them, he was known to be the cynical one. Many times, his distrustful attitude worked in their favor because it made them more cautious with certain business transactions but they didn't want the negativity today.

"Son, we don't need this shit right now. Alejo tried to shut us down but we're back in business. I call that a win for us."

"Listen, I have a reliable source who told me Alejo is now supplying some crew from New York," Clayton told them.

"What does a New York crew have to do with us?" Kasir wanted to know.

"They recently set up shop right here in Houston."

"That motherfucker!" Allen pounded his fist down on the marble top table. "I should've known he had someone in place to move our product when he cut us off. He wants to completely dry me out. Sonofabitch!" he barked.

"Dad, if there were no other drugs on the market for buyers to choose from then what we have would be suitable for now. But if another crew is in Houston serving Alejo's product, we'll be fucked if we can't compete," Kasir sighed.

"I told you I have someone who can get us great

product for a decent price. If you give me the clearance I can make it happen. Give me a chance to show you what I can do, dad." Clayton implored.

Kasir and Clayton both sat anxiously like they were kids again. Waiting eagerly for their father's approval. Clayton had become used to always coming in second place to his older brother but it didn't stop him from trying to gain his father's respect.

"Okay, Clayton. Do what you have to do," Allen said. This huge weight seemed to be lifted off Clayton's shoulder. "Kasir, try to get rid of the product we have as quick as possible. We'll use the money for Clayton to purchase the new drugs. Do we also have some money left over from the last buy?"

"Yes," Kasir nodded. "He gave us a huge discount, hoping we would do long-term business."

"Okay, well give that money to Clayton."

"Dad, thank you for this opportunity. I won't let you down," Clayton promised.

"You better not or you'll be taking the loss on this," Allen warned his son. "I'll be out for the rest of the day. I can be reached on my cell. But the two of you should be able to handle things without me."

"I guess you'll finally have your chance to prove yourself, baby brother," Kasir remarked, loosening his tie.

"That's all I ever wanted. I hope you don't feel slighted for me asking dad to let me use my plug."

"Listen, if you can get us prime product then show me what you can do. I'm not convinced but like dad said, it will be your loss."

"Thanks for the support, big brother," Clayton said

sarcastically.

"Whatever…right now I'm more interested in why dad is taking the rest of the day off. Does he have plans with mother?" Kasir asked.

"No. I'm sure his plans are with someone else." Clayton let slip.

"Excuse me? What the hell does that mean?" Kasir questioned angrily.

"Mother made me promise not to say anything."

"I don't care what you promised. You better tell me what the fuck is going on with our mother," Kasir demanded.

"Dad is having an affair."

"You a lie!" Kasir yelled.

"Keep your voice down. We do have a building full of employees."

"These doors are soundproof. Now tell me what is going on with our mother…now!"

"I told you. Our father is having an affair," Clayton repeated.

"Dad would never cheat on our mother. I don't believe you." Kasir stood up becoming agitated.

"You mean you don't believe mother because that's where the information came from."

"So, mother told you this?"

"Yes!"

"Why would mother confide in you?"

"Because unlike you and dad, she values my opinion and respects me as a man," Clayton boasted. "What are you doing?" he asked when Kasir reached for his phone.

"Calling mother. I want to hear this from her," Kasir seethed.

"Don't you dare!" Clayton reached his hand out and grabbed the phone from Kasir's hand.

"Give me my fuckin' phone!" Kasir roared.

"I'm not giving you shit until you calm the fuck down. I promised her I wouldn't say anything. That means you can't say shit," Clayton spit.

Kasir frowned up his face, furious. The idea of his father cheating on his mother almost seemed implausible to him. She was the love of his life. No other woman could compare. Their marriage had always been goals for him but had accepted a long time ago he would probably never obtain it. Now within a matter of a few minutes the fairy tale had been shattered. Kasir was feeling like the child who discovered Santa Claus doesn't really exist. He's simply a created character. He didn't want to believe his father was flawed.

"How long do you plan to stay in Houston? Is this long-term?" Alejo was taken aback by what Damacio was telling him.

"Yes. I'm relocating there. I'm opening a new club. I found the perfect venue and they've already started renovations."

"I get it now!" Alejo's eyes widened with approval. "You want to be closer to Caesar and his crew to keep an eye on them. Very smart, son." He patted Damacio on his shoulder.

"Thank you." Damacio didn't dispute his father's assessment. If it kept him off his back, then so be it. If his father knew the truth, that he was moving to be with a woman he'd falling hard for, he would never hear the end of it.

"I have a good feeling about Caesar but you can never be too cautious. I mean look what a traitor Allen turned out to be," Alejo scoffed. "You being right there in Houston, you'll be my eyes and ears," he grinned.

"Yes. Have you heard anything else from Allen? I've said it before but I think you made a major mistake cutting him off and keeping his money."

"Fuck Allen! He choked me in my own home. He almost killed me."

"How did you expect him to react? You kept his product and his money. You do know at some point he's going to retaliate." Damacio felt his father was being way too lax about the entire situation. He wasn't sure if he was getting even more stubborn with age or if the liquor had him not giving a fuck.

"Please! Allen has turned into a corporate prude. Ten years ago, I would be preparing for retribution but this new Allen, he'll try to write it off on his taxes like those rich white men he plays golf with do," Alejo joked.

"You're not worried so neither will I be," Damacio shrugged. "I have a few more things to take care of before I leave. Ernesto is going to be overseeing my businesses here. But you know I'm always available for you." Damacio hugged his father.

"I'm going to miss you, son. When are you leaving?"

"At the end of the week."

"Have you already found yourself a place to live?"

"Yes. I'll have you come visit once I'm situated."

"Of course, you will. Maybe you'll find a wife while you're there too. I need a grandson," Alejo announced.

"I know, dad. You remind me every other day."

"Because it's important. If you have no heirs who will be left to carry your legacy. Children is what makes the world go on. They give you hope for the future. You must give me a grandson...ideally a few. I know you'll make me proud, you always have, Damacio."

"I have to go. I'll call you later." Damacio hugged his father one last time before leaving out. He wasn't ready to discuss it with his dad but marriage and starting a family had been heavy on Damacio's mind lately. It was all due to his relationship with Ashton. He found himself wanting to spend every minute of each day with her but he knew she wasn't ready to be a mother. Ashton was young and enjoyed partying too much. Marriage yes but babies was a no, at least for now.

"Girl, I still can't believe you living in Houston now! It's a major change from NYC though...right!" Vannette said as her and Brianna were getting pedicures.

"Yeah but I'm liking how laid back and chill it is. I think the slower pace is making Caesar wanna settle down," Brianna smiled.

"For real?! You might be right. He did move you down here. I remember a few months ago you was stressing."

"Yeah, when that nigga told me he was leaving New York, I thought we was done. Remember, I had been dealing wit' him for like two years."

"I know!" Vannette smacked, taking a sip of the Moscato that came with her deluxe pedicure package. "I remember when you first started dealing with Caesar. It was right before I moved down here for school."

"Then you understand, I put my time in wit' that nigga and he was bouncing without me. But I guess he realized these chicks down here can't compete wit' a bitch like me," Brianna bragged.

"I know that's right! You sounding mighty confident over there."

"The other day, he dropped what would equal a down payment for a luxury car on a shopping spree for me. You see this purse," Brianna pointed to the rose, brown, and grey Yves Saint Laurent python tote. "That's just one of the many things he bought me."

"Damn, he got any friends. I need a rich dude too," Vannette pouted.

"Girl, you too cute not to have a nigga wit' some money. You been out here for a minute and you still ain't got no man?"

"I mean I'm dealing with this one dude but he like legitimate rich. His family got super long paper."

"Word! How you meet a nigga like that?"

"I go to school with his sister and we're pretty close. Ashton...I told you about her."

"Yeah...yeah. The girl you be calling the princess."

"Yep, that's Ashton," Vannette laughed. "I met Clayton through her. But he ain't serious about me. He probably gonna end up with one of those debutante type bitches."

"So, why are you wasting your time wit' him?"

"Because he's fine, can fuck, and we do go to nice places," Vannette nodded.

"I feel you."

"But a bitch do have bills and I want nice things like that python bag you got."

"Well, Caesar the top dog, so he making the most paper. Since he already taken, I would suggest you either fuck wit' Jeff or Darius. Those are his number one and two guys."

"Out the two of them which one is more likely to come off some paper?" That was Vannette's only concern.

"I would say Jeff. Darius comes off as a little stingy to me."

'I don't need that headache, so scratch Darius off the list."

"Then Jeff it is. I'll set up a double dinner date for us. It's time I get you out this struggle life," Brianna winked.

"Thanks, babe. I'm glad you're here with me. I have a feeling things are about to start looking up!" Vannette beamed, blowing her friend a kiss.

Chapter Sixteen

All Lies

"Yeah, I Said It" by Rihanna was the perfect background music as Crystal and Kasir wasted no time picking up right where they left off, inside each other. The sounds of oohs, aahs, and moans of pleasure were silenced by the melodic beat echoing through the bedroom. Instead of going out for the long overdue dinner date Kasir promised her, Crystal opted for them to stay in and have a sexual workout that was turning into an all-night marathon.

"I'm starting to think you're using me for sex,"

Crystal turned to Kasir and said. "But I don't mind," she teased.

"I was just thinking the same thing." Kasir let out a slight laugh, kissing Crystal on her shoulder. "I had dinner reservations for us but..."

"But my idea was much better," Crystal cut in and said, placing her index finger over Kasir's lips. "Don't you agree?"

"I do but there's one problem."

"What's that?" Crystal sat up in the bed and asked.

"I was hungry before and now I'm starving. We still need to eat dinner. Do you feel like going out?"

"How about we order in and have dinner in bed," Crystal suggested.

"We can do that," Kasir said getting out of bed. "Let me go in the kitchen and get some takeout menus. I'll be right back."

"Okay." Crystal was about to lay back down but heard her phone ringing. "Gosh, I thought I put it on silent," she huffed walking over to her purse to retrieve her cell. "It's Allen," she mumbled, debating if she should step out and call him back. *How would I explain it to Kasir? But Allen hates when he can't get in touch with me and I can't fuck that relationship up. What should I do?* Crystal debated with herself.

"Is everything okay?" Kasir's question shook Crystal out of her thoughts.

"Umm, everything is fine."

"Whatever you were looking at on your phone seemed to have you in deep thought."

"I was just reading a text from Remi. She has some

girl emergency. Do you mind if I step out on the balcony and call her back?"

"No, go right ahead," Kasir said. "I'll order us something to eat. Is there anything in particular you want?"

"Whatever you decide is fine," Crystal said, hurrying outside to make her call. "Allen, hi," she said closing the glass door.

"Is there a reason you missed my call?"

"I was actually at the library studying for a test I have tomorrow. My phone was on do not disturb. I just realized you called."

"When will you be home?"

"In about an hour. Are you coming over?"

"No, not tonight. I need to spend some time with my wife. But send me a text when you get home. I'll call you tomorrow."

"Okay. Have a good night." When Crystal went back inside, Kasir was sitting in the chair by the fireplace.

"You get things straight with Remi? Or do you need to leave?" Kasir asked looking up at Crystal. She was standing in the doorway wearing his shirt and seemed surprised by his question.

"She's good. False emergency...so what did you order?" Crystal came over to Kasir and gave him a kiss. She was being extra playful as if nothing was wrong. She kneeled down beside him, laying her head on top of his leg.

"I hope you know I'm not a dumb man, Crystal, and you don't have to lie to me."

"Kasir, where is this coming from?"

"From the second I came back into the bedroom

and you were holding your phone, shits been off with you. And don't tell me it's because of Remi. Do you have a man? If so, then own up to that shit but don't lie to me like I'm stupid."

"I know you're not stupid. I'm the stupid one." Crystal bit down on her lip, pissed at herself for playing things like a rookie. But that's what happens when you start catching real feelings for someone.

"Then tell me what's really going on with you."

"I'm having an affair with a married man." Crystal made the disclosure so hastily, it took Kasir a minute to respond.

"Is that who you went outside to call?"

"Yes," Crystal admitted putting her head down before continuing. "I didn't want to call him but if I didn't, I knew he would be upset."

"But it's okay to upset me instead."

"I didn't mean it like that."

"Save it." Kasir pushed Crystal off of him and stood up.

"This is why I didn't want to tell you the truth. Because I couldn't stand the idea of you looking at me like this."

"Like what? A side chick who doesn't even value herself enough to get a man who isn't already taken," Kasir scoffed.

"Pretty much," Crystal said sadly. "We've spent all our time having great sex that we don't even know anything about each other."

"Save the bullshit excuses."

"That first night we slept together was supposed

to be it! You were never supposed to try and get in touch with me and I was never supposed to call you but I did!" she yelled.

"Why don't you just leave," Kasir said, walking out his bedroom.

"I don't wanna leave. I want to be here, with you."

"I've never shared a woman in my life and I'm damn sure not about to share you with a married man."

"Kasir, you have to understand. A few months ago, I was basically homeless sleeping on Remi's couch. I've been a screw up my entire life. Meeting this man was the best thing that ever happened to me until I met you. You're both so similar in many ways, except even though I know you're too good for me, you never make me feel less than."

"So, what, this other man makes you feel like shit but because you think he's better than you, that makes it okay?"

"You make it sound simple but it's not. He doesn't know he's making me feel like shit. But I do because it's draining trying to stick to some bullshit script and be somebody that I'm not."

"Are you even in school? And that day I ran into you, were you really coming from a job interview or were those nothing but lies?"

"All lies. My life has been one big lie for the last few months. But if you let me, I can tell you about the real me or don't you care anymore?" Crystal wondered if Kasir could hear her heart racing as she waited to hear his response.

"I'm glad you're both home!" Ashton beamed seeing her mom and dad sitting in the living room, listening to classical music and drinking wine.

"Come give your father a hug," Allen said putting his hands up. "I feel like I never see you anymore."

"I know but you're always at the office, out of town, or a late night meeting," Ashton said, giving her father a warm embrace before giving her mother a hug and kiss too.

"This is so nice. I thought I was going to have a lovely evening at home with my beautiful wife but now my beautiful daughter will be joining us too. Have a seat, Ashton," Allen smiled lovingly at his daughter.

"Sure, as long as you don't mind me pouring a glass of wine. I know you always have the best, daddy!"

Allen laughed as Ashton filled her wine glass all the way to the rim while her mother simply shook her head. Karmen knew her daughter was a mess but she couldn't help but be amused by the free-spirited beauty.

"I really wanted to talk to both of you about something," Ashton said sitting down on the sofa across from her parents.

"We're listening," Allen said, leaning back in his chair.

"Vannette is getting a place off campus. She asked me to be her roommate and I agreed."

"You're moving out?" Karmen put her glass down,

feeling blindsided. "I thought you loved living here with your father and I."

"I do but I'm not a teenager anymore. I can't live here forever. I think it's time for me to live on my own," Ashton explained.

"You know you're my princess and I'll miss having you here but if you want to move out, then you have my full support."

"Thank you, daddy!" Ashton ran over to her father and gave him a huge hug.

"Allen, I can't believe you're agreeing to this."

"Karmen, we adore her but Ashton's not a little girl anymore. I think it's great she feels ready to be on her own," Allen said to his wife.

"Mom, I know after Clayton and Kasir moved out, you were hoping I would live here forever. It's time for me to spread my wings but I promise to come visit often," she said sweetly.

"You better come visit often...I'll miss you so." Karmen felt her eyes watering up. "Well, I guess we better find you a beautiful place to live because no daughter of mine will have anything less."

"Actually, Vannette already found a place."

"Really...where?" Karmen wanted to know.

"She found a condo in the Memorial area."

"Memorial...how can Vannette afford an area like that?" Karmen wondered.

"Her uncle has a close friend who needed to sublet his place immediately and gave her a really great deal," Ashton lied and said.

"Wow, that must be some deal. I can't wait to see it."

"Mother, you know I'll invite you over as soon as I get settled in."

"I can at least take you furniture shopping. I'm sure you want everything to be brand new."

"Can you believe it's already furnished. All I have to do is move in," Ashton smiled.

"Well honey, you're no freeloader. Let me get my checkbook," Allen said getting up from his chair. "You can pay your portion of the rent up for a year and give Vannette a little extra and do whatever you want with the rest."

"Thanks, daddy. I'm sure Vannette will appreciate it."

"Are you sure this is what you want to do?" Karmen asked her daughter once Allen was out of the room.

"Yes! I'm positive. Please be happy for me because I'm super excited."

Karmen could see the enthusiasm written all over her daughter's face. She wanted to be happy for her but Ashton had been the last bit of glue holding her marriage together. With her daughter leaving the nest, there wasn't much reason left for Karmen to fight to keep her family intact.

Chapter Seventeen

Vices

Caesar was sitting at the round table in the five-star restaurant, wondering how in the hell Brianna convinced him to agree to this double date shit. His right hand man, Jeff, wasn't even making the dinner tolerable because he was too busy gassing Vannette, trying to guarantee he would be getting the pussy tonight. He glanced over at Brianna who was reapplying her liquid lipstick so she could take a quick pic for the gram. Caesar had been contemplating when he would send her back to New York but he kept pushing it back because he hated sleeping alone.

At one time, Caesar was addicted to sex. But soon after he began hustling, he traded one addiction in for another, making money. So, although sex was no longer his top priority, he wasn't able to detach himself from needing a warm body next to him. Having that helped Caesar sleep better at night. But it had to be someone he knew wouldn't try to fuck him over which made his selections limited. With that being the case, Brianna was his only option, at least for now.

"Caesar, you didn't compliment me on my new dress. I got it yesterday," Brianna said while still posing for her camera phone.

"Oh, my fuckin' goodness," Vannette said tapping Brianna on her leg.

"What is it?" Brianna asked while trying to take one last picture.

"Ashton just walked in with a dude we saw at this club in Miami a couple months ago. He was with that Instagram model Shanice Monroe. That sneaky bitch," Vannette giggled.

That tidbit of information got Brianna off her phone. She wanted to see who Vannette was talking about. "Damn, he coming in here wit' security...what that motherfucker do?"

"I don't know but it must be some major shit."

"Is Ashton the chick you be calling princess?" Brianna questioned.

"Sure is. Her father is Allen Collins. Some huge business mogul. You should see their crib. It's some palatial estate type shit," Vannette popped. "Let me go over and say hi to my friend. I'll be right back."

Brianna wanted to run off with Vannette and be nosey but she knew Caesar didn't play that shit. He would have her ass on the next plane back to LaGuardia Airport if he thought for a second she was being disrespectful. She wasn't about to do anything to mess up her situation.

"Ashton, hey girl!" Before Vannette could even hug her friend, two men who were suited up blocked her path.

"She's my friend. It's okay," Ashton said standing up to give Vannette a hug. "Hey girl! It's good to see you. Babe, this is my friend Vannette."

"It's a pleasure to meet you." Damacio stood up and shook her hand before sitting back down.

"Girl, he so fine!" Vannette whispered in Ashton's ear. "I see why yo' ass been missing in action lately."

"I know and he's amazing in bed," Ashton smirked. "But I'ma call you tomorrow. There's something I need to run past you."

"Cool! Well enjoy the rest of your evening and it was nice meeting you," Vannette waved at Damacio after exchanging air kisses with Ashton and going back to her table.

"So, what did she say?" Brianna wasted no time asking when Vannette got back to the table.

"I definitely got vibes they were a couple. She said she was going to call me tomorrow so I'm sure I'll get all the juicy details."

"Did you find out what his job occupation was that required the extra security?" Brianna inquired.

"No, but I'm mos def gonna ask her tomorrow.

They serious about they job too because at first I couldn't even get to Ashton. I'm like this dude the president of what!" Vannette joked. "I can't wait to find out who he is though."

Caesar sat back listening but he already knew the answer to Vannette's question. What he couldn't believe was Alejo's son was dating his enemy's daughter. He couldn't see either men being cool with that. Caesar wasn't surprised Ashton was attached to her own drug kingpin...like mother, like daughter.

"Baby, do we always need security when we go out? They practically went for my friend's neck," Ashton complained. "And they're blocking my view. I can't see anything."

"The only view you need to see is me. But I am sorry about your friend. It's for your own protection."

"Protection from what, you're not in Miami anymore."

"My club here will be opening up in a couple weeks. It's going to bring a lot of attention to me and you. I explained all this to you," Damacio stated with impatience in his voice.

"I know, I'm just..." Ashton paused mid sentence, reaching in her purse for a pill. She quickly swallowed, washing it down with champagne.

"Do you think it's wise to mix a narcotic with alcohol?"

"It's not a big deal and it makes the sex spectacular. You should have one too."

"I don't do drugs." Damacio grabbed Ashton's hand as she was reaching back inside her purse to get another pill. "And I don't need to be on something to enjoy sex with you."

"Damacio, I didn't mean it like that. You know how much I love having you inside of me. Why are you looking at me like that? Don't fuck up my high."

"Ashton, how long do you plan on poppin' pills and drinking? Eventually you'll have to give that up. You can't carry my baby if you're always high."

"Carry your baby?!" she looked at him stunned.

"Yes, you don't ever want to have kids?"

"I just never thought you saw me as a woman you'd want to be your baby's mother."

"I don't. I see you as a woman who would be my wife and the mother of my children."

"Really?" she didn't seem convinced.

"Yes. You're the only woman I can see myself spending the rest of my life with."

"I love you so much." Ashton leaned over and kissed Damacio. She was ready to have sex with him right there on top of the table in the restaurant. "You turn me on so much."

"Is that you talking or the pills?"

"Damacio, would you stop!" Ashton pouted. Folding her arms.

"I want you to start easing off the pills."

"You make it sound like I'm some sort of drug addict. All my friends pop pills and none of us are junkies."

"There is such a thing as a functional drug addict.

They go to school, hold down jobs. Their life seems perfect, until they no longer have access to the pills they're used to taking. It's not until then that they realize they're an addict."

"Before my parents sent me away to boarding school, I went to a prep school and once a month we had these huge pill parties. Everyone would bring prescription drugs they got from their parents or bought from dealers. We would put them in a big bowl and try different ones. We had a blast. I grew up thinking that's just what rich kids do, no biggie. None of the kids seemed like addicts. Now you're telling me you want me to stop."

"You can't do that for me?"

"When you stare at me with those dark, hypnotic eyes, it's hard to say no."

"Then don't."

"Babe, listen." Ashton placed her hand on top of his. "How about I only pop a pill or two when we go out partying and no other time?"

"Okay, we can do that for now. But, Ashton, you have to decide if you eventually want to be my wife and the mother of my children. Not only do I have an obligation to my father but also to myself, to bring an heir into this world to carry on my family's legacy."

"I've heard my father talk to my brother's about continuing on the family legacy more times than I can count. So, I get it but I need some time."

"You're still so young. I understand the resistance and I won't force you to do anything you don't want to do."

"But I want you more than I could ever want any drug. You are my drug. I just need some time to let the other one go."

"I'll give you the time you need."

"Thank you. I truly can't imagine my life without you."

Damacio and Ashton's lips once again allied, kissing each other like obsessive lovers. In their worlds, only the two of them existed. But would their love survive when reality set in.

"We're very pleased with the product. I think we can do long-term business under one condition," Clayton said locking eyes with his connect, Jeevan.

"What is that?"

"You come down on the price."

"Clayton, I already give you the best price. What more do you want from me?"

"Come on, Jeevan. Your father is one of the biggest Indian crime bosses. His organization is described as the Goldman Sachs of organized crime. He dabbles in everything from counterfeiting and arms running to extortion. I even hear he dabbles in the film industry and financed several popular Indian films. From my understanding, he derives a substantial amount of revenue from Bollywood."

Jeevan let out a hefty laugh. "Clayton, you must not believe all the rumors. Because my father married one of those Bollywood actresses doesn't mean he finances them too. Everything else you named might be accurate. But I won't confirm anything," Jeevan said with amusement.

"There is plenty of revenue being made in Mumbai. I just want to be able to do the same here, for my organization," Clayton stated.

"Your organization? I was under the impression that you worked for your father under his organization?" Jeevan pointed out.

"The same way you're branching out making moves, I want that for myself."

"I don't follow." Jeevan seemed puzzled.

"I know you've been operating your drug business behind your father's back. Ravi Budesh is the one who oversees your father's massive drug operation. I would prefer to continue getting my drugs directly from you instead of going through him. But if you don't come down on your prices, you'll leave me no other choice."

Clayton knew he was playing a dangerous game by insinuating that he would go over Jeevan's head and deal directly with the person his father put in charge. He was basically threatening to expose Jeevan for his underhanded deals. Jeevan could've easily taken offense but Clayton was hoping his quest for money and power would trump that.

"Clayton, what goes on in my country has nothing to do with what I'm doing here with you. I have no desire for you to deal directly with Ravi. I can offer you product and prices which suits both our needs."

"Very good because once I take over for my father,

I plan to expand the operation. I will be needing much more product and I plan to make you my go to man."

"I like that," Jeevan nodded. "To bigger, better, and more lucrative deals," he smiled, shaking Clayton's hand.

The two continued to exchange their drug enterprise ambitions in Jeevan's Presidential suite at the Magnolia. Many called this the best boutique hotel in Houston with its modern aesthetics and vibrant colors. But Clayton thought it was the best because he'd just closed the most lucrative deal of his life. Before meeting with Jeevan, he'd been warned Jeevan's father was known for being a ruthless leader. But that didn't stop Clayton from jumping at the opportunity to break bread with his son.

Clayton had one agenda and that was taking over from his father. He didn't care so much about running A. C. Enterprises, he was even willing to hand it over to his brother Kasir. But moving drugs was a different conversation. He longed for the day he would get the fear, respect, and power that came with being a notorious drug kingpin. Clayton knew aligning himself with a man like Jeevan would put him closer to his objective.

Chapter Eighteen

PSSY Management

"I was shocked when I got your phone call to meet you here," Caesar said, when he sat down in a booth at the nightclub. "It always amazes me how different clubs look at night opposed to the day," he remarked.

"I say the same thing," Damacio nodded. "But I'm rather pleased how this place has come together, especially in such a short period of time," he said looking around.

"I take it this must be your club?"

"You are correct."

"What about Miami?"

"What about it?"

"It takes a lot of time to get a club off the ground. That would be hard to do if you're still based in Miami."

"Miami will always be home for me but I needed a change."

With your family being there, I'm surprised you would want to move, unless Alejo sent you down here to keep an eye on me."

"My father thinks very highly of you, Caesar. He believes you and the organization you run will make him a lot of money. He doesn't need me to watch you. I have my own reasons for moving to Houston."

Caesar nodded his head as if he considered what Damacio said to be the truth. "One man to another, I'll take your word."

"I invited you here because I wanted to let you know I would personally be handling all of your business transactions. There is no need for you to reach out to my father, you come to me."

"I'm assuming Alejo is aware of this?" Caesar asked.

"Of course. My father is the leader of the cartel. All decisions go through him. I would not have asked you here if he hadn't given the ok," Damacio made clear. "With that said, I also wanted to personally invite to the opening of my club on Friday. I hope you will come and feel free to bring your friends."

"No doubt. I will be here. I know you're new to Houston and so am I, but I've been here a little longer," Caesar grinned. "If you need a date for your grand opening, I can provide one for you."

Damacio laughed slightly. "Thank you but I'm good. I'm in a relationship."

"Sounds serious."

"It is." Damacio stated.

"I see. Last week I had dinner at a restaurant over on Westheimer. I saw a man who I could've sworn was you but at the time I figured I was wrong, since you lived in Miami. Now that I know you're here...was that you?"

Damacio paused before speaking. Caesar's question sounded simple enough but he knew there was an underlying reason he asked but didn't know why. "Unless I have a twin, then yes that was me. Why didn't you come say hello?"

"Again, I figured I was mistaken. Plus, you were with a woman so I didn't want to interrupt."

"I was having dinner with my girlfriend but next time, come speak."

"I will."

"Give me a minute, Caesar. I need to speak to the gentleman who just walked in," Damacio said excusing himself.

"Take your time," Caesar nodded. He wanted a moment to take in what he'd confirmed. Damacio wasn't merely dating Allen's daughter, they were in a serious relationship. He could only imagine the rage Alejo would feel if he knew his prized son was sleeping with his enemy's daughter. For now, Caesar thought it best to keep the information from Damacio's father. He didn't want a war to break out between the two men until he got what he wanted first...Karmen.

"Wait until Damacio sees me in this," Ashton beamed, admiring herself in the dressing room mirror, wearing a peony nude balconette bra in embroidered tulle with the matching thong.

"We're supposed to be looking for something to wear to your boyfriend's club, so why are you trying on lingerie in La Perla," Vannette rolled her eyes.

"I am wearing this to the club but it's going to be under my dress," Ashton winked. "I'm giving my man some eye candy with my clothes on and off."

"Fine. But can you hurry up. I want to make it to the Prada store before they close."

"Prada?! Where you get Prada type money from?" Ashton inquired while taking off the lingerie so she could put her clothes back on.

"I told you about Jeff. The guy Brianna hooked me up with."

"You've only been talking to him for a couple weeks now and he already giving you Prada type money. Dang, girl, I see why you left Clayton's stingy ass alone."

"I haven't left Clayton alone, he just hasn't been able to see me lately. He claims he's busy with work. I guess being a big time executive is time consuming," Vannette smacked.

"You don't need Clayton. You have this new dude and clearly he likes you."

"Girl, he's a drug dealer. He's making a shit load of tax free paper. Giving me money to spend at Prada is equivalent to buying a meal at McDonalds for him."

"Vannette, you a fool!" Ashton laughed.

"I'm serious. Plus, the only reason he's been dropping bread is because I haven't fucked him yet. I have to thank Brianna for schooling me to that."

"What, your friend told you to hold the pussy hostage?" Ashton frowned up her face.

"Yep, and the shit is working."

"A guy can spend lots of money on you and become your man even if you don't make him wait on the panties. I didn't hold my pussy hostage with Damacio."

"Bitch, you rich. You don't have to pussy manage like us broke chicks," Vannette sighed. "Brianna has taught me, what's between my legs is my best asset, so I need to negotiate accordingly."

"I hear you. Let me go pay for this stuff and get out of here. I know you wanna hit Prada," Ashton giggled as she walked off.

Vannette did consider Ashton a friend but also envied the girl she labeled a princess. She would prance around spending her daddy's money and now she had found a man who was not only good looking but also didn't seem to be hurting for paper. She wanted that life for herself. Although she wouldn't admit it, Vannette secretly hoped Clayton would be the one to make her dream a reality.

"If you're here to gloat, save it," Kasir scoffed when

Clayton walked in his office.

"What do I have to gloat about," Clayton taunted, taking a seat on the leather chair.

"I was wrong. Is that what you want to hear? Father can't stop singing your praises after you came through with the new product. It's as good or dare I say even better than the drugs we were getting from Alejo," Kasir conceded.

"Then why isn't that frown turning into a smile. You should be pleased."

"You're right. You came in and saved the day like Superman," Kasir joked. "On the real, we're back in business. It was shaky there for a minute. After Alejo royally fucked us, I wasn't sure we were coming back from that."

"I told you both that old fuck was crazy. I guess it took this bullshit for you to hear me though."

"Maybe but I have other things on my mind. I went to see mother yesterday."

"Did you mention what I told you to her?!" Clayton jumped up in a panic.

"Calm down, Clayton and have a seat. I didn't tell mother anything. I was hoping she would bring it up to me but she spent the entire time talking about Ashton."

"Ashton...what has our sister done now?"

"Nothing. Our mother is experiencing empty nest syndrome," Kasir shrugged.

"Wait, Ashton moved out?"

"Yep. She got an apartment with Vannette."

"Interesting."

"Vannette hasn't mentioned it to you?"

"I've been busy so I haven't really spoken to her."

"That's all mother wanted to talk about was how much she missed her precious Ashton. Do you think with Ashton being gone, it will bring our parents closer or make things worse?" Kasir's distress over their parent's marriage was growing.

"I don't know what's going to happen but our mother is a lot stronger than you think. Whatever transpires, I put my money on her coming out on top," Clayton stated.

"This isn't a game, little brother. Our mother and father have been husband and wife for over twenty years. If they don't make it, I might give up on the whole idea of the institution of marriage."

"I gave up on the idea of marriage a long time ago," Clayton divulged. "Ever since Adam and Eve bit the apple, a man and woman in love will eventually destroy each other."

"Gosh, Clayton, you always have to be so fuckin' contemptuous."

"Just speaking the truth, big brother. A few years from now, after some woman you wanted to spend the rest of your life with breaks your heart, you'll finally be able to admit I'm right," Clayton stated confidently, before exiting out of his Kasir's office, leaving him in deep thought.

"Baby, let me show you this dress I got today for the

grand opening of your club!" Ashton said excitedly. She pulled out a deep teal, floor length dress with thigh high slits on both sides. It had a dramatically cinched waist and twinkling beaded straps. "What do you think?"

"I think it's beautiful but I already picked out a dress for you to wear to the party." Damacio went in one of the bedroom's walk-in closets and stepped back out with a brushed gold, second skin gown, cutout at the waist to reinforce an hourglass silhouette.

"OMG, it's gorgeous!" Ashton gushed, tossing the dress she bought on the floor and ran over to grab the one Damacio got for her. "Baby, it's perfect." She held the dress up to her body, twirling around in front of the floor length mirror.

"You will be the most beautiful woman there, but that goes without saying." Damacio stood behind Ashton, sprinkling kisses on her bare neck. He began caressing her breasts, letting his fingers press down on her hardened nipples.

"Before you start undressing me, so you can blow my mind in bed, I wanted to tell you something."

"Can it wait until after I fuck you and make love to you at the same time?" Damacio whispered in Ashton's ear.

"It really can't. I told my parents I was bringing my boyfriend over for dinner Saturday."

"You what?" Damacio stopped making love to Ashton with his hands, immediately ceasing all foreplay.

"I don't want to hide our relationship from them anymore. I want them to meet the man who stole my heart. Are you not ready to meet them?"

"I just wish you would've discussed it with me first."

"I knew you would only try and talk me out of it."

"Why would you think that?" Damacio asked.

"Because I know you would love for us to stay in our own world forever. I would love that too but I hate lying to my parents. After I bring you to dinner and they see how incredible you are, then I can tell them the truth. I'm not living with Vannette but with you," Ashton said caressing Damacio's face.

"I would love to have dinner with your parents. I can personally thank them for creating you."

"Then we have a busy weekend, my love. Your party on Friday and dinner with my parents on Saturday."

"Yep, but right now I want to focus on today," Damacio said laying Ashton down. They didn't even bother making it to the bed. The sex was just immaculate right there on the marble floor.

Chapter Nineteen

In Da Club

"I was so surprised when you called but I'm glad you did," Vannette told Clayton, while having pillow talk after an intense sex session. "I've missed you," she happily admitted, laying on his chest in bed.

"I missed you too," Clayton somewhat lied. He did enjoy the sex with Vannette but not so much that he missed her. He had a roster of women that he equally enjoyed having sex with because Clayton faithfully wore a condom with each of them. So, all the pussy basically felt the same to him. Some got a little wetter than others and since he never tasted the pussy, the wetness was an individual per basis thing. What made each chick stand out from the rest was how magnificent their head game was. If Vannette didn't hold the number one position, she mos def was top three. She had an exceptional head game, so Clayton did miss that.

"For real," Vannette smiled, happy to hear those words from Clayton. "You know how much I care about you...right?"

"I wanna believe you but I'm not sure I can," Clayton said stroking Vannette's hair.

"How can you say that?" Vannette lifted her head up. "All I do is wait for your calls."

"Then why didn't you tell me you moved off campus and got an apartment with my sister?" Clayton asked the question but he highly doubted it was true. Instead of playing the guessing game, he decided to go directly to the source.

"Because I didn't!" Vannette blurted out, not wanting to ruin what she hoped might be a chance of having a real relationship with Clayton.

"You don't have to lie to me, Vannette," Clayton said calmly. "If you're seeing someone else and you don't want me to know because they're paying your bills, I won't be mad. I have to respect that since I know I've been too busy to give you what you need." Clayton knew exactly how to play Vannette and she fell right in line.

"I only want to be with you. Anybody else I'm seeing is just to buy time until you're ready to settle down," she confessed like a girl in love. "Ashton is living with her boyfriend. She only told her parents she was living with me so they wouldn't go crazy."

"Ashton has a boyfriend?"

"Yes!" Vannette nodded. From the baffled look on Clayton's face she could tell he wasn't convinced. "I swear! She met him when we went to Miami for spring break. I guess you can call it a whirlwind romance."

"If she met him in Miami, how are they living together here in Houston?" Clayton questioned, getting more information from Vannette than he expected when he invited her over.

"From what Ashton told me, he owns several nightclubs. He had some in Miami and now he's opening up one here in Houston. The grand opening is actually tomorrow. He seems to be some major figure."

"What makes you think that?"

"I ran into her at a restaurant last week and he had security with him."

"Security...and he owns nightclubs? Do you know his name?" Clayton was curious why a man who owns nightclubs needed to walk around with security.

"Damacio something...I don't know his last name," Vannette shrugged.

Clayton's body felt like it froze up after Vannette dropped the name. He tried to keep his cool because he didn't want her to know all the thoughts sprinting around in his mind. He didn't believe in coincidences. The same Damacio he knew owned nightclubs and lived in Miami had to be the one Ashton was playing house with. This spelled trouble on every level and Clayton wasn't sure how he needed to address the newfound information.

"Yo, I look so fuckin' hot in this, don't I babe?" Brianna asked Caesar who wasn't paying her any attention. But she really didn't need him to cosign on what she already knew. Brianna was completely feeling herself in the latte colored Gucci jumpsuit. It was super snug with a playful off shoulder design. The front had a deep plunge with cutout tethered by looped cord detail. The ankle cutouts gave even more flash of skin which Brianna loved.

"You almost ready to go?" Caesar questioned, putting on some cologne as he stared at his reflection in the bathroom mirror.

"Almost. Let me dab a little more Trophy Wife on my cheekbones," Brianna said coming into the bathroom where Caesar was.

"I'm feeling your whole look...very sexy," he smiled.

"I knew you would when I tried it on at the store. This jumpsuit, plus the Fenty makeup and my fresh silk press got me looking like a scrumptious snack," Brianna boasted.

Caesar continued smiling, watching Brianna add the final touches to her makeup. There was no denying her sex appeal but unfortunately for Brianna a pretty face and plump ass was no longer enough to hold Caesar's attention. He saw himself as a boss and wanted a woman who reflected that image. To him, Brianna didn't make the cut but he intended to keep her around until he had the woman he envisioned to fill the spot.

"Baby, the club looks incredible! I'm so happy for you." Ashton beamed, running her fingers through Damacio's thick, wavy hair as she pulled him in for a kiss.

"Be happy for us. Any success I have, I want to share it with you."

"I'm so in love with you. I can't wait for us to get home, so I can show you just how much." Ashton caressed Damacio's earlobe with her tongue, then licked the inside which she knew got him so aroused.

"You know how much that drives me crazy," he moaned.

"I can feel how much it drives you crazy too." Ashton pressed her body against his and placed her hand on Damacio's hardened dick. "We could always go into your office and I can pleasure you right now," she teased whispering in his ear.

"Be a good girl," Damacio said, sliding his hand up Ashton's dress. There's a massive crowd coming in and I have to make sure all is being run smoothly. I promise to blow your mind when we get home."

"I know you will, baby."

"Your table is set up for you in the VIP area. I already told the hostess to bring your friends over when they arrive," Damacio told Ashton.

"Thank you, baby," she kissed him again.

"I put a few bottles of champagne on your table, for you and your friends but try not to drink too much. I don't wanna have to kill somebody because you get drunk and start flirting with some random dude."

"I won't...I promise." Ashton blew Damacio a kiss and as she headed to the VIP table she noticed her friend Lizzie come in. She ran up to her high school bestie excited to see her.

"Omigosh, Ashton! I'm so happy to see you. You look amazing!"

"So, do you. I was afraid you weren't going to make it, since I gave you such last minute notice."

"Please! I was looking for an excuse to leave Boston for a few days. I was thrilled when you called," Lizzie smiled.

"Great! Come on, you already know what's about to go down," Ashton said taking her friend's hand and leading her to their table. "The bubbly is already waiting for us."

"I would expect no less from the ultimate party girl."

"Isn't that your friend who just sat down?" Brianna asked Vannette, looking a few tables over.

"That sure is Ashton. I love the dress she's wearing but it's not the one she picked out when we went shopping," Vannette commented, wondering where she got it from.

"Who is the white girl sitting with her?"

"I don't know," Vannette shrugged. "Probably one of her friends from boarding school. She still keeps in touch with a couple of them. I'll be back. I want to find out where she got that dress from," Vannette said getting up.

"Wait for me!" Brianna called out to Vannette as

she hurried off. She turned around looking for Caesar and saw him at the other table talking with Darius and Jeff. "Hey!" she said interrupting his conversation.

"What is it?" Caesar barely looked up to acknowledge Brianna.

"I'll be over there with Vannette," she told Caesar and he simply nodded his head and continued talking to his partners.

Brianna was glad Caesar was preoccupied. She only told him where she was going to be ladylike. She knew Caesar preferred women who seemed classy so recently, whenever she could remember, she'd try to play the role. Brianna wasn't a bird but more so fake bougie, which was one of the reasons she was determined to befriend Ashton.

From the first time Vannette spoke about her friend she called a princess, Brianna wanted to meet her. She thought when Vannette mentioned she was going shopping with Ashton the other day, she would invite her to go too but nope. She was beginning to think Vannette didn't want them to meet. So, when Brianna saw Ashton sitting only a few tables away from them, she wanted to take advantage of the opportunity.

"Vannette, there you are!"

"Oh, hey. I told you I was coming to speak to my friend."

"You ran away so fast, I must didn't hear you," she smiled. "I'm Brianna and you are?" she turned her attention to Ashton who was already on her third glass of champagne.

"I'm Ashton and this is my bestie Lizzie!"

"Hey ladies!" Brianna waved. She caught the frown on Vannette's face when Ashton introduced Lizzie as her bestie. Brianna figured it was the title Vannette wanted for herself.

"Ashton, I really need to go to the ladies' room," Lizzie said taking her hand.

"Come on, I'll show you where it is." Ashton led the way, holding another glass of champagne in her hand.

"I really need to use the bathroom too," Brianna said to Vannette. "Come on, let's go."

"I'm straight," Vannette said still frowning.

"Okay. I'll be back." Brianna rushed off to catch up to the women. By the time she got to the restroom, Ashton and Lizzie seemed like they were in the mist of having their own party.

"You sure you don't want a hit?" Lizzie asked Ashton who was playing with her hair in the mirror.

"I'm positive. I promised Damacio I wouldn't go overboard tonight."

"You promised Damacio," Lizzie laughed. "You must really like this guy."

"I do...I love him," she admitted to her friend.

"What?! I've never heard you say that about a guy before."

"Because I've never felt like this."

"Wow, I'm happy for you but you're still missing out on some excellent coke," Lizzie teased.

"I guess one line wouldn't hurt," Ashton giggled.

Brianna watched as Ashton stood there in her brushed gold gown, draped in diamonds, looking like a movie star. It seemed surreal watching her do coke right in front of her eyes.

"Do you want some?" Lizzie offered as if noticing Brianna's presence for the first time.

"Thanks for offering but I'm good." Brianna then went into one of the stalls and pretended to be using the restroom but instead she listened as the two women chatted it up. They were reminiscing about previous occasions they partied together and all the fun they had. When she heard them about to leave, Brianna came out so they could walk out together.

"Ashton, I love your dress. It's gorgeous," Brianna complimented her as they left out the bathroom.

"Thanks, my boyfriend got it for me. Speaking of my boyfriend, here he comes now. I'll see you ladies back at the table," Ashton said walking towards Damacio, greeting him with a kiss.

"I was looking for you. Your friend said you went to the bathroom," Damacio said holding her close. "Are you having a good time?"

"The best, even better now that you're holding me."

"Are you high?" Damacio held Ashton's arms firmly and stared her in the face.

"No silly! I just had a few glasses of champagne so you can calm down."

"Then what the fuck is that white powder under your nose?!" he barked, holding her face tightly.

"Okay, so I had one line of coke. It's not a big deal," Ashton snapped, pushing Damacio's hands away.

"I make one simple request of you but you can't

even do it. You had to go get drunk and high!" Damacio shouted.

"Stop being so dramatic! I'm not fuckin' high! I only did one freakin' line," she shouted back.

"Spoken like a true coke whore," Damacio spit.

"Fuck you!" Ashton belted, swinging back her arm and slapping the shit out of Damacio as her hand connected to his face. His initial reaction was to choke her up but he didn't give into his rage. Instead he walked away before things went all the way left. Ashton continued screaming at Damacio before deciding to head back to her table.

From a distance, Caesar watched as the drama had unfolded between Damacio and Ashton. Although he couldn't hear what was said, their body language spoke volumes. He wasn't expecting for Ashton to swing on him and wondered what had gone down between the couple. He also noticed as she was coming back to the VIP area that Ashton seemed out of it. Before he could give it further thought, shots rang out. It sounded like machine guns were raining bullets throughout the club. The combination of glass shattering, people scrambling, and ear-piercing screams took the pandemonium to the next level.

Caesar was about to take cover under one of the tables but noticed while everyone else was trying to hide, Ashton seemed to be in la la land. She was looking around as if fireworks were going off instead of a hail of gunshots. He then spotted one of the shooters aiming his gun in Ashton's direction. Caesar jumped on top of the table before leaping over several chairs to push her out the way. If it had been one second later, Ashton's torso would've been riddled with bullets.

His breathing was rapid and heart thumping as Caesar's body continued to shield Ashton. She seemed to be oblivious to what was going on until she noticed a man lying in a puddle of blood next to her. That's when panic set in.

"Omigosh, we're gonna die!" Ashton cried.

"Shh!" Caesar put his finger over Ashton's mouth. "Calm down, I got you." He scooted them towards one of the booths so they could get out of the line of fire. Caesar could feel Ashton's body trembling. He knew she had every right to be scared because he wasn't sure how they would escape the chaos. Then as quickly as the gunfire erupted, it ceased just as swiftly.

Everyone in the club remained frozen in their positions, too scared to move. After a few more minutes, all the lights in the club came on and you could sense the relief in the air.

"Ashton! Ashton! Ashton!" Damacio's voice was echoing through the club. But Ashton didn't answer, she was still in shock, not able to say a word.

"Over here!" Caesar stood up and called out to Damacio. He was still keeping an eye on Ashton who was bent over in the fetal position. "She's under the booth," Caesar told Damacio when he got closer.

"Baby, are you okay...are you hurt?" Damacio asked, wrapping his arms around Ashton.

"I thought I was gonna die," Ashton finally said, coming down from her high. "I would've, if that man hadn't pushed me out the way. It was like I couldn't move," she mumbled still shaking.

"I'm sorry I wasn't there for you but I'm here now and I'm taking you home." Damacio helped Ashton up and she buried her face in his shoulder. "Was it you that pushed her out the way?" Damacio asked Caesar who was still standing nearby.

"Yeah, she just needed a lil' help." Caesar tried to keep it casual not wanting Damacio to make a big deal out of it.

"I will forever be grateful," Damacio stated, locking eyes with Caesar.

"I will too," Ashton lifted her head and said. "Thank you for saving my life."

"Come on, baby. Let me take you home."

Caesar watched as the couple disappeared out the back exit. He was dying to ask Damacio what the fuck happened and who shot up his club but it was evident his only concern right now was Ashton, which he respected. Caesar decided to wait before flooding Damacio with questions, although he was certain of one thing. The ramifications of what happened tonight would be nothing less than deadly.

Chapter Twenty

About Last Night

Damacio held Ashton's naked body close to his all night. He never wanted to let her go. Damacio felt guilty for not protecting the woman he loved. He felt he should've had at least two bodyguards watching over her. His decision could've cost Ashton her life and it would've if not for Caesar. Knowing that had Damacio barely able to sleep. So, when his phone started ringing, he quickly answered.

"Hello."

"Son, you must come to Miami!" Alejo's hefty voiced roared through the phone. "They shot up my home and killed several of my men, including Gilberto!"

"Father, you're not hurt, are you?" Damacio asked while gently moving Ashton's body out the way, trying not to wake her.

"No! I was able to escape without harm but I cannot go back to my home. I'm leaving for Mexico but before I leave, I need you here. We must retaliate immediately."

"Do you know who's responsible?"

"Of course," Alejo scoffed. "I know it was Allen."

"You're positive?"

"Just get to Miami. We will discuss when you get here." The phone went dead and Damacio realized his father had hung up.

"Baby, get back in bed," Ashton called out as she turned over.

"I have to go to Miami. It's a family emergency."

"What?!" Damacio's announcement woke Ashton out her sleep. "You can't leave me...not after what happened last night."

"Baby, I know but I'm going to have a few of my men stay here and watch over you. You'll be well-protected."

"I don't want them here. I wanna be with you. Let me come to Miami with you...please," she begged.

"Ashton, I would but it's too dangerous."

"Dangerous? Is somebody after you...is it the same people who shot up your club?"

"I'm not sure, that's why I have to go to Miami. I'll be back as soon as possible. I promise," Damacio said kissing Ashton, whose eyes stared up at him with fear and sadness.

Clayton was on his way out for his morning run when he heard someone at his door. He looked through the peephole and saw it was his brother. "What the hell is he doing here?" he said out loud, turning off the alarm before opening the door.

"Kasir, you better have a good reason for delaying my morning run," Clayton said letting his brother in. "Why you look stressed out? It's too early for anything bad to have happened."

"Man, I need a drink," Kasir gasped, sitting down.

"You need to tell me what the fuck is going on. I ain't never seen you act this frazzled." Clayton was bewildered.

"Dad finally called in that favor with them Haitian shooters."

"What?! To take out Alejo?"

"Yes," Kasir nodded.

"Really!" Clayton smiled. "I'm surprised and impressed. I thought dad had lost his edge."

"Apparently not but don't celebrate yet. The Haitians fucked up. Alejo is still alive. You know what that means."

"Slow down. Alejo may suspect dad was behind the hit but he doesn't have proof."

"Alejo doesn't care about proof. He's been itching for an excuse to go to war with our father, now he has one," Kasir sighed. "This isn't going to end well."

"Does dad seem worried?" Clayton asked.

"No. He's pissed the Haitians didn't finish the job but other than that he seems unbothered."

"Then you need to stop worrying, big brother. Hell, Alejo bleeds just like everybody else. Next time, they'll have to get it right."

"If there is a next time. I'm sure Alejo is going into hiding."

"He can't hide forever," Clayton reasoned.

"I don't know, this just feels real bad to me." Kasir was becoming antsy again. "Maybe dad went too far. He even had this club Damacio recently opened shot up. I didn't even know dude was in Houston."

"When was Damacio's club shot up?"

"Last night. Dad had them boys doing double duty. Hitting up Miami and Houston simultaneously. Talk about making bold moves," Kasir shook his head.

"Have you spoken to Ashton?"

"Ashton? I'm trying to have a discussion with you regarding business and you bring up our sister."

"Just answer the question."

"No, I haven't spoken to Ashton. Now can we get back to discussing what's important," Kasir said with infuriation.

"This is important," Clayton said dialing Ashton's phone number but it kept going straight to voicemail. "Fuck! Answer your phone," he barked.

"Why are you so pressed to get in touch with Ashton?"

"I'll explain in the car. Come on, let's go!" Clayton said grabbing his keys.

"Last night was bananas!" Brianna exclaimed, as she was preparing to cook breakfast "Thank goodness, I had to go back to the restroom. If I'd been out there when the shooting popped off, I probably would've pissed on myself outta fear," Brianna told Caesar while he sat at the kitchen table flipping through the newspaper.

"Yeah that shit was outta control. Them niggas had a lot of balls coming in Damacio's club, showing out like that."

"Who you telling! I'm only surprised more people didn't end up dead after all those gunshots I heard."

"I have a feeling what happened last night were warning shots. A prelude to some bigger shit about to go down. All that ammo them boys had, they could've taken out a lot more people."

"Yeah, Vannette told me they almost took out Ashton. Luckily, you were there to save her. I'm sure Damacio would've never forgiven himself if his girlfriend died at the opening of his club."

"No doubt. She was scared to the point of being completely out of it," Caesar said thinking about how things played out last night.

"I'm sure Ashton was scared but I think being high was the reason she was completely out of it," Brianna shrugged while scrambling some eggs.

"High, you mean drunk?"

"No, I mean high. Ashton and her friend was snorting coke in the bathroom right before that craziness broke out."

Caesar took his eyes off the paper and looked over at Brianna. "Are you sure?" Caesar had already peeped Brianna was a little jealous of Ashton. He wanted to make sure she wasn't just talking shit instead of spitting facts.

"I'm positive. I saw it with my own eyes. I was shocked. Ashton comes across so put together and perfect. Clearly, she's not. Trust me, you were definitely her angel in disguise because she would've been shot dead in the middle of the club, if not for you."

The more Caesar learned about Ashton, the more he realized the only thing mother and daughter shared in common was their beauty. Karmen was reserved and exuded class while her daughter was a free spirit who seemed to enjoy living on the edge. Caesar couldn't help but wonder if Damacio was playing with fire by making Ashton his woman.

Chapter Twenty-One

Over My Dead Body

"I wasn't expecting you until much later but I'm always happy to see my baby girl," Karmen beamed, hugging Ashton.

"I'm happy to see you too, mom. I've missed you so much."

"You know you can always move back home. This house feels empty without you."

"It felt empty even when I was here because it's too damn big," Ashton mocked.

"True but you know your father, the bigger the better. Enough about that, how are you? I can't wait to meet your boyfriend tonight. Bernice is preparing a wonderful dinner with all your favorites," Karmen said with enthusiasm.

"About that. We have to reschedule the dinner." Karmen could detect the sadness in her daughter's voice.

"Why? You seemed so excited about us meeting him. Did something happen?"

"I was...I mean I am excited about you and dad meeting him. An emergency came up and he had to go away for business."

"Hopefully we can reschedule soon. Right now, I'm more concerned about that gloomy look on your face. What's the matter?" Karmen asked, getting up from her chair to go sit next to her daughter on the couch. "You know you can tell me anything, Ashton."

"Mom, I..."

"Thank goodness you're okay!" Clayton ran in the living room and held his sister. "I've been trying to call you and your phone kept going to voicemail."

"I haven't had a chance to charge my phone," Ashton told him.

"Hey mom," Kasir walked in a few minutes later, giving her hug.

"Kasir! It's so good to see you. I have all my kids here with me at the same time. This is turning out to be the best Saturday I've had in a very long time."

"We're glad to be here with you," Kasir smiled.

"Thank you but Clayton why did you rush in here so panic stricken, relieved your sister was okay?" Karmen wanted to know.

Clayton and Ashton were always taking jabs at each other. Most of the times they seemed to be at odds but deep down, Clayton adored his sister. If anything happened to her, he would lose it. So, when Kasir told him about Damacio's club being shot up, he thought the worse.

"I'll let Ashton tell you." Clayton and Ashton exchanged stares and she knew what was up.

"Mom, the boyfriend I was telling you about, opened a club last night. While I was there, some men came in and shot the place up," Ashton divulged.

"What! Omigosh!" Karmen immediately grabbed her daughter, cuddling her tightly. "I'm so glad you're okay. You must've been terrified."

"I was." Ashton admitted becoming choked up. "I came this close to being killed."

"Dear God!" Karmen put her hand over her mouth, horrified how close she came to losing her only daughter.

"Ashton, I'm so sorry you went through that," Kasir said solemnly.

"Me too," she said putting her head down. "A stranger saved my life. He didn't have to risk his life for mine but he did."

"Are you serious? Do you know who he is? We have to thank him and I'm sure dad will want to show his generosity."

"I know his name, it's Caesar. Vannette is close to his girlfriend. I definitely plan on calling him later on today to thank him again."

"You said his name is Caesar?" Karmen questioned,

having a feeling it had to be the same man she knew. It wasn't like the name Caesar was common, especially in Houston.

"Yes. Thank goodness he was there or I would be dead right now."

"Ashton, don't think about that." Karmen held her daughter again.

"Mother's right. You're alive and here with us. Nothing else matters," Clayton stated.

"Ashton, have you told mother who your boyfriend is?" Kasir inquired.

"Your sister was actually bringing him over for dinner tonight so we could meet him. Now I understand why you had to cancel. Ashton, are you sure you want to be in a relationship with a man who's having shootouts at his club? I mean what sort of things is he involved with?"

"Mother, he owns several nightclubs. Most of them are in Miami. This is his first one in Houston. It was probably some jealous guys who see him as competition and they're trying to put him out of business," Ashton explained, defending her man. "You know how people can be. It's not Damacio's fault he's successful."

"Damacio?" Karmen shot a glare at both her sons. "That's an interesting name."

"He's Spanish. I know dad wanted me to marry a distinguished, wealthy, African American man like him but destiny had other plans. Damacio is it for me. I know when you both meet him, you'll fall in love with him too."

"You're in love with him?" Karmen's voice cracked

when she asked the question.

"Very much so. I never thought I could feel this way about any man but he's everything to me. I can't wait for you to meet him. Hopefully he won't be in Miami long," Ashton said standing up. "I'm starving. I'ma get something from the kitchen. I'll be back."

"Please tell me your father wasn't the one that had Damacio's club shot up last night," Karmen said to her sons once Ashton was gone.

Kasir and Clayton both put their heads down answering their mother's question without having to say a word.

"Do either of you know if Damacio is aware who Ashton is?"

"I only found out this morning they were even in a relationship, so I have no idea what Damacio knows," Kasir replied.

"And you, Clayton?"

"I found out a few days ago from Vannette. I planned on telling you but it was such a sticky situation. I didn't know how to handle it. But if I'd known dad had planned to go on the attack against Alejo and Damacio I would've spoke up sooner," Clayton sighed.

Then, at what seemed to be the worst time, Allen Collins walked through the front door. Karmen's first instinct was to scream at her husband for almost getting their daughter killed, although unintentionally. She also wanted to tell him not to explode, once he found out who Ashton had planned to bring home for dinner. Instead, Karmen opted to zip it.

"Did I walk into the wrong house because I've

never heard my family be this quiet before," Allen joked.

"Hey dad. We were discussing some business, that's all," Kasir spoke up.

"I hope nothing too deep, especially since I saw Ashton's car out front. Where is she?" Allen asked. His daughter only knew him as being an upstanding, successful businessman and he wanted it to remain that way.

"She's in the kitchen," Clayton told him.

"I'm assuming with the frowns on each of your faces, Kasir informed you about my retaliation against the Hernandez clan."

"Yes. I wish you would've given us a heads up, dad," Clayton said.

"I normally try to keep you boys in the loop but this required me to move in silence."

"Well, your silence almost got our daughter killed," Karmen scoffed.

"What in the world are you talking about?"

"Ashton was at that club last night and one of those bullets almost hit her. She could've died, Allen."

The color seemed to drain from Allen's face. Never would he deliberately put his daughter's life in jeopardy but that's what he'd done.

"Daddy, you're here!" Ashton came back in the living room, ecstatic to see her father. "I had a rough night, daddy. I need for you to give me one of your superman hugs."

"Whatever you need. I'm always here for you." Allen squeezed his daughter so tightly, wanting to suppress his overwhelming guilt. "I'm so sorry for what happened to you. I wish I could erase it."

"It's okay, daddy. You're here now and like always you make everything better." Ashton kissed her father on the cheek.

"I love you so much," he said.

"I love you too. I wish I could stay longer but I have some things I need to take care of before Damacio gets back. I can't wait for you to meet him, daddy."

Allen's body tensed up just hearing the name Damacio but never did he think his beloved daughter was speaking of his enemy. "I'm looking forward to meeting him too, although I wish he had a different name," he joked.

"I know, I know. Like I told mother..."

"Ashton, we don't have to talk about that now," Karmen said cutting her daughter off. "Go take care whatever you need to and I'll call you later on to see how you're doing," she said trying to rush Ashton off.

"Sounds good!"

"Wait." Allen reached out and took his daughter's hand before she could walk away. "Tell me more about Damacio."

"He's amazing, daddy. You would've met him tonight if he didn't have to go out of town. He didn't tell me but I think it has to do with the club shooting last night."

Karmen, Clayton and Kasir all had a grimaced expression on their faces. When Allen told Ashton to tell him more about Damacio, they knew he had already figured out the truth but needed it validated.

"Dad, I think Ashton needs to get going," Clayton

said, wanting to diffuse what was coming next.

"Mind your business, son." Allen warned, pointing his finger at Clayton.

"Am I missing something? Why do you seem upset, dad?" Ashton questioned.

"Because I am. Is this boyfriend you've been talking about, Damacio Hernandez?"

"Yes. Why do you say his name with such disgust in your voice?"

"He's a drug dealer, Ashton! I didn't give you the best of everything so you could waste your life on a criminal!" Allen roared.

"He's not a criminal! He's the owner of several nightclubs. You think because some monsters came into his club and shot it up, he must be a criminal. The only person who's a criminal is the person responsible for what happened!" Ashton shot back.

"I think we all need to calm down. We can discuss this later," Karmen said putting her arm around Ashton to walk her to the door.

"No! We will discuss this now!" Allen barked. His tall, well-built body towering over his wife and daughter. "I forbid you to ever see Damacio Hernandez again. Don't speak that man's name in this house."

"Why are you doing this?" Tears swelled up in Ashton's eyes. "Mom..."

"Oh, baby, it'll be okay."

"I'm in love with him, daddy."

"Don't you dare say that!" Allen got all up in his daughter's face and barked. Ashton had never seen her father so angry. She stepped back out of fear.

"Allen, that's enough!" Karmen stepped forward and yelled. "Don't you see what you're doing to our daughter. This conversation is over until you can calm down."

Allen stood breathing like a bull. His rage was unbearable. No one wanted to be in the room with him right now.

"Mom, I have to go. I'll call you later," Ashton said before storming out.

"Don't!" Karmen cautioned her husband. "Let her go."

Both Kasir and Clayton chose to remain silent. They were used to seeing their father enraged but never had it been aimed at Ashton. Their entire lives, she could do no wrong in their father's eyes, so to see him out of control like this, they knew it was best to stay out his way.

"Did you know about this, Karmen?" his accusatory tone was off putting to say the least.

"No. I only found out right before you."

"I should've let those Haitians kill him when they had the chance!" Allen balled up his fists and scoffed.

"Did you not hear what our daughter said...she's in love with him."

"Don't say that!" he flung his arm up, dismissing her words.

"If you make Ashton choose, you will lose." Karmen's words cut Allen deeper than any knife ever could.

"You don't know that."

"Yes, I do. I had dreams of performing lead with the

New York City ballet at the Lincoln Center and it could've happened. But I met you and fell deeply in love. I knew I couldn't have both, so I gave up my dreams of becoming a ballerina, to be with my first love. I know that look Ashton had in her eyes. She is in love with Damacio. As much as you hate to hear that, it's the truth. Just like I chose my first love, our daughter will do the same."

"Over my dead body," Allen said looking at his wife before leaving.

Chapter Twenty-Two

Lies and More Lies

Alejo Hernandez was nestled away on a private paradise called Little Palm Island. It was a few miles off Overseas Highway in Little Torch Key, near Key West but it felt like a secluded, self-contained universe. That was exactly how he wanted it. Alejo had a home there for many years but only his most trusted security detail and closest family members knew about it. He'd purchased the luxury cottage on the beach for times like this, when Alejo knew his life was in imminent danger.

    "Damacio, you've proven yourself to be a loyal son

by arriving so soon," Alejo stated, taking in the breeze from the water by the white sand beaches.

"I'm always loyal to you, father. You should know that by now."

"After seeing my life flash before me last night, I don't know anything anymore. I can't believe Gilberto is dead. He's worked for me since before you were even born. This is a dark time for me and it will only get worse."

"My clubs in Miami and the new one in Houston were also shot up. Unfortunately, a few people were killed but there could've been a lot more casualties. Have you confirmed who's behind the hit?" Damacio asked.

"It was members of the Haitian mob but I know it was Allen who ordered it."

"I didn't know Allen had connections with the Haitians. Are you sure? They don't take orders from him. The Haitians move a lot of product in Miami and we've had problems with them in the past."

"My gut tells me it was Allen and my gut is never wrong."

"Is that your gut or guilt."

Alejo turned to his son. "Where's the respect. How can you speak to me like that?"

"Father, I respect you but I'm a man and I speak to you with truth. I told you there would be consequences for what you did. You can't steal millions from a man without ramifications."

"How can you defend him?! My son, standing in front of me, defending my enemy!" he yelled.

Damacio lowered his head, disheartened his father wouldn't admit his actions ignited the flame. "I ask you this. If Allen had stolen from you, what would you have done?"

Alejo stared off gazing up at the clear sky. He'd come outside to bring himself a little peace, on a day full of dejection but the dark cloud had followed him. Instead of taking responsibility, Alejo fought back.

"Are you quick to defend a spineless man like Allen Collins because you're sleeping with his daughter?"

"Excuse me?!"

Alejo left his son standing on the front porch and went inside. Damacio was tempted to follow him but instead sat down on the rocking chair to further ponder what his father said. He knew Ashton's last name was Collins but that wasn't uncommon so he thought nothing of it. Now he had to wonder, but that was short lived.

"Ashton has grown into a beautiful woman, just like her mother," Alejo commented handing his son multiple pictures of the two of them together in Houston.

"You had me followed?"

"You're my son. I was concerned about you. You've always loved Miami. Then out of nowhere you decide to move to Houston. I wanted to see what was going on with you."

"Then you should've asked, not hired someone to follow me around and invade my privacy," Damacio seethed, tossing the photos down.

"I did ask and you lied to me. You said you wanted to keep a closer eye on Caesar but it was really for this young lady. I only met Ashton one time when she was a very little girl. Allen was always so protective of her. I can only imagine his fury, when he finds out his only daughter is sleeping with a man he despises. Or maybe he already knows," Alejo raised an eyebrow. "Maybe this hit had nothing to do with those stolen millions you speak of but revenge for you bedding his precious daughter."

"Enough of the speculation," Damacio scoffed. "Unlike you, I doubt Allen has someone stalking his daughter, regardless this will become a problem because I have no intention of giving Ashton up."

"Then work with me, son. A dead man's opinion holds no weight. You'll be free to have a life with Ashton, if Allen is out the way permanently. "

"You want me to help you kill the father of the woman I love?"

"I'm doing you a favor, son. I'm helping you kill Allen before he kills you. Trust me, I know the man. He'll never allow you to be with his daughter. Is your relationship with Ashton worth dying for or killing for? You think about it. The choice is yours, Damacio."

"Jeff, hold up for a second, let me answer this," Caesar said, curious to know who was calling him since he didn't recognize the number. "Hello."

"Hi, this is Karmen. Do you have a moment to talk?"

"Talk about a pleasant surprise. Of course, I have a moment. As many as you need." Caesar left his theater room and went upstairs for some privacy.

"I might be wrong but I doubt it. I was calling because I wanted to thank you for saving my daughter's life."

"You're welcome. How is she doing?"

"She's still shook up but after what she went through, it's to be expected."

"No doubt. I hope she never has to go through anything like that again," Caesar said.

"Me neither. She's my baby girl. I don't know what I'd do if anything happened to her."

"Nothing will, at least if I'm around."

"Good to know Ashton has a guardian angel."

"I have to admit, I was surprised to find out you have a grown daughter. You look too young."

"Then you'll be even more surprised to know I have three grown children. My daughter and two sons. Sometimes I can't believe it myself."

"Your husband is a lucky man. I'm also lucky because you kept my number. I was worried you'd tossed the business card I wrote it down on in the trash."

"I was tempted but now I'm glad I didn't. If I had, I wouldn't have been able to call and thank you. I mean..."

"Mrs. Collins!", Karmen stopped mid-sentence when she heard Bernice knocking on her bedroom door.

"Come in, Bernice. Caesar, can you hold on for one second?"

"Sure."

"Mrs. Collins the hospital just called. It's Mr. Collins, he's been in a car accident."

"Oh gosh! This can't be happening. Is he okay?" Karmen exhaled, fearing the worse.

"I'm not sure, Mrs. Collins. Would you like for me to drive you to the hospital?"

"No, you stay here. I'll drive myself. I'll be down shortly. Thank you," Karmen said closing her bedroom door. "Caesar..."

"I know, you have to go. I hope your husband is okay."

"I appreciate that. Bye."

"Karmen!" Caesar called out before she could hang up.

"Yes."

"Keep my number close and feel free to use it anytime."

"I have to go."

A wide smile spread across Caesar's face when he got off the phone with Karmen. She was fighting it but he knew she was becoming more drawn to him. Caesar never considered himself a patient man but he was willing to sit back and wait for Karmen to give in to temptation.

"Hi! My housekeeper spoke to someone here who said my husband had been brought in. His name is Allen. I believe this is the correct hospital," Karmen said to the lady at the front desk, trying not to sound flustered but it wasn't working.

"I'm sure you're concerned but try to calm down. You said his name is Allen, what's the last name?"

"So sorry, Collins...Allen Collins."

"No need to apologize. Yes, Mr. Collins was brought in."

"How is he? I was told he was in a car accident. Was he hurt badly?"

"You will need to speak to his nurse but you can go see him," the lady said, giving Karmen the room number and pointing in the direction she needed to go.

First Ashton, now Allen, I don't know how much drama I can take in one day. Please Dear God let him be okay, she thought to herself hurrying to where his room was located. As Karmen was rushing down the hall, she stopped mid step. A familiar face made her freeze. She first noticed the driver Allen used frequently and he was escorting Crystal out. But before her husband's mistress got on the elevator they locked eyes. A wrath of fury unfamiliar to Karmen surged through her body. It was so powerful that it frightened her for a second. She took a deep breath and regained her composure before going into her husband's room.

"Karmen, what are you doing here?" Allen lifted himself up while lying in the hospital bed.

"Someone from the hospital called the house and spoke to Bernice. They told her you had been in a car accident, so of course I came to check up on you," Karmen said sweetly.

"Well, I'm happy to see your beautiful face. Come sit down," Allen smiled.

"How are you doing?"

"I'm fine. I have some pain and a few bruises but other than that I'm good. The doctor is being overly cautious. They ran some tests and want to monitor my condition overnight. But I'll be home first thing tomorrow morning," he said placing his hand on top of his wife's hand.

"Be sure to send me that new address so I can have all your personal belongings delivered there for you," Karmen said flipping Allen's hand off of hers.

"Karmen, what are you talking about?" Allen questioned completely dumbfounded. "Is this about Ashton and Damacio?"

"You disrespectful fuck!"

In all the years they had been married, Allen could count the number of times he heard his wife curse and it was never at him.

"Karmen, you need to calm down. What has gotten into you?!?" Allen tried to get out of bed but realized there were a bunch of tubes hooked up to him. "Listen, sit back down and tell me what is going on."

"The only place I'll be sitting down with you at is our attorney's office, for a divorce settlement agreement."

"Baby, please talk to me. I've never seen you so upset. We've been married for over twenty years. Why would we ever get divorced?"

"Save it!" Karmen popped. "Your mistress was in the car with you, when you got in that accident. What... after we had a difference of opinion this afternoon you went and got your ego and dick stroked by her."

Allen was left speechless by what his wife said, which was definitely a first for him. So, he did what most men do when they find themselves in this predicament...deny.

"Karmen, you're my wife and I love you more than anything in this world. I'm not having an affair and no woman was in the car with me when I got in an accident."

"You might've been convincing if I didn't have the receipts, you sonofabitch. It's good to know how easily you can look me in the face and lie," Karmen fumed.

"I'm not lying!" Allen stuck to his lie with a straight face.

"So, Crystal just so happened to be leaving with your driver. Before you continue to lie, the private investigator I hired months ago has all the information I need to bury your ass in divorce court. Now that I think about it, maybe I'll have your shit shipped to the corporate apartment you have your mistress stashed at."

"Karmen, please! I...I..." Allen knew at this point he needed to choose his words carefully.

"Don't come home tomorrow because the locks will be changed." Karmen grabbed her purse and bolted. All Allen heard was the clicking sound of her five inch heels down the hall.

Chapter Twenty-Three

Transparent

"So how are things going between you and Jeff?" Brianna asked as her and Vannette were having lunch.

"It's going pretty good. He's starting to get stingy with the money, though. I guess it's because I haven't fucked him yet," Vannette shrugged, while she continued to eat her fried cauliflower with cranberry & mint.

"Hold up, you still ain't fucked that nigga? I told you to make him wait, not starve his ass," Brianna rolled her eyes.

"I know but honestly I don't want to fuck him period," Vannette confessed.

"Why? Jeff ain't the finest nigga but he ain't the ugliest neither," Brianna smacked. "He's actually kinda cute. Especially since he always dresses nice, keeps a fresh haircut, and of course them pockets heavy."

"It's not that. He's definitely fuckable."

"Then what is it?" Brianna put her elbows on the table and leaned forward waiting for the answer.

"I've been seeing Clayton again."

"Ashton's brother?"

"Yes." Vannette said with a twinkle in her eyes.

"I thought you said he didn't take you seriously and figured he would end up with one of those rich debutante type chicks."

"I did but I spoke too soon. The few times I've seen him things were different."

"Different how?" Brianna pried.

"I can't explain it. We seemed to connect more than on just a physical level. OMG! Speaking of Clayton, he just walked in," Vannette said nervously. "Don't turn around, he's coming this way," she mumbled under her breath.

"Vannette, how are you?" Clayton said kissing her on the cheek.

"I'm great," she grinned. "I'm surprised to see you here." That wasn't exactly true. Vannette remembered Ashton mentioning Brennan's of Houston was one of Clayton's favorite restaurants.

"I love this place. The food is amazing and the ambience is nice too. I'm actually here for a business meeting with a client. My apology, how rude of me. I'm Clayton and you are?"

"Brianna. I've Vannette's friend from New York."

"We have to take you out and show you a good time while you're here visiting," Clayton said with charm and ease.

"She's not visiting. Brianna lives here now with her boyfriend," Vannette was quick to add.

"I see. Well, I'm entertaining a couple of potential clients tonight. Why don't the two of you join us," Clayton suggested.

"Sure, we'll come," Vannette agreed extra giddy.

"Wonderful. I'll call you later on with the details." Clayton gave Vannette a goodbye kiss before turning to her friend. "Nice meeting you, Brianna."

"Nice meeting you too."

"Are you sure Caesar won't mind you coming out tonight?" Vannette asked after Clayton left.

"Caesar will be fine with me going out with you. He told me earlier he had business to handle tonight," Brianna lied. The truth was, she had dealt with enough men to know when they were ready to replace you. Brianna hoped she had finally found the one with Caesar but lately, he had been showing all the tell-tale signs he was no longer interested. She knew he would be trying to ship her back to NYC any day and she had no plans of returning.

Brianna was loving Houston and all it seemed to offer. Her intention was to stay by any means necessary. That meant latching on to another man and Clayton was too enticing to pass up. She understood why Vannette was hung up on him and it just wasn't because of his good looks. The man oozed power and class. There was nothing new money about Clayton and Brianna wanted a taste of that life.

"Mrs. Collins, your husband is at the front door," Bernice said, coming into the home gym room.

"Did you let him in?"

"No. I did as you told me and wouldn't let him in. However, Mr. Collins said he wasn't leaving until he spoke to you."

"Bernice, call 911 and tell them we have a potential intruder who needs to be escorted off the property."

"Mrs. Collins, are you sure you want me to do that?" the housekeeper's reluctance made Karmen reconsider.

"You're right, that wouldn't be a good idea. Allen has a lot of police on his payroll. Let him in. Thank you, Bernice," Karmen said pausing the elliptical machine. She had no interest in seeing her husband but she also knew how stubborn he could be. If he said he wasn't leaving until he spoke to her then that's what he meant.

Karmen could hear Allen speaking with Bernice in the living room. She stopped in the kitchen and got a bottle water before making her way to where he was.

"There you are. Karmen, thank you for seeing me," Allen said looking freshly released from the hospital.

"Bernice, can you give me a moment alone with my husband."

"Of course, Mrs. Collins."

"You have five minutes and then I want you gone."

"I deserve this coldness from you. Marriage vows are sacred and I broke ours. But, Karmen, please believe I love you. You're the love of my life. You're the only woman I want to spend my life with."

"Can you get to the point because I have things to do," she said with ice in her voice.

"I met Crystal a few months ago when I was having drinks at a bar I frequently visit downtown. She reminded me so much of you. Not physically but her interests and topics we discussed. I felt at ease, something no other woman besides you made me feel. I got caught up and I'm sorry."

"You got caught up...is that the best you can do?" Karmen was unimpressed.

"Baby, what I'm trying to say is I made an unforgiveable mistake but don't let that destroy our marriage and what we've built. My relationship with Crystal is over. I've already told her and made arrangements for her to move out of the corporate apartment. You have always been my first priority and nothing or no one is going to come between us. I'm begging you, Karmen, to please give me one more chance. I will spend the rest of my life making this right."

"Fine, Allen. I'll give you one last chance. If you betray me again, this marriage is over."

"Damacio, you're home!" Ashton said, running up to him when he entered their bedroom. "I was going crazy without you."

"I'm sorry I had to leave you."

"Were you able to take care of everything you needed?"

"Not everything, but enough. I need to talk to you about something," Damacio said, sitting Ashton down on the bed.

"So, do I."

"You go first."

"Are you sure?"

"Yes. You've been through a lot the last forty-eight hours. You deserve to go first." Damacio kissed her lovingly.

"I went to see my parents yesterday. To tell them we wouldn't be coming over for dinner. When I told my dad about you, he flew into a rage and started spitting all sorts of lies about you. He said you were a criminal and drug dealer." Ashton got up from the bed becoming angry all over again.

"Baby, it's okay. Don't get yourself worked up."

"No, it's not okay! The only reason he's flipping out is because you're not black. My father wanted me to marry a man just like him and honestly for the longest time I wanted to. He was my hero. I looked up to him and I still do. But I'm not in love with a black man, I'm in love with you."

"And I love you but what your father said about me is true." Damacio wanted to be transparent. "I am a criminal and a drug dealer. My father is Alejo Hernandez and he is the head of a major cartel. His home was shot up and so were my clubs in Miami and of course the shooting here in Houston. The Haitians were responsible but my father believes your father ordered the hit."

"Why would my father put a hit out on you and your father? That doesn't make any sense."

"Because your father is in the same line of work as we are." Ashton turned to him in disbelief. "You know I would never lie to you."

"I guess I'll end up marrying someone just like my father after all."

"Are you saying you're ready to marry me?"

"Have you changed your mind about wanting to marry me?" Ashton questioned.

"Never."

"Good, then let's go to Vegas tonight and get married."

"Are you serious?" Damacio stood up and grabbed Ashton by the waist, pulling her close.

"Very serious. By tonight I want to be Mrs. Damacio Hernandez."

"Than you shall be. I'll make the arrangements," Damacio said kissing his future wife.

Chapter Twenty-Four

A Favor For A Favor

"Is your friend still coming? I wanted to introduce her to one of my associates," Clayton told Vannette as they sat in the booth drinking champagne.

"Yes. We were supposed to come together but she got held up. She said she would meet me here. Let me call her." As Vannette was reaching for her phone she saw Brianna walk into the lounge. She felt some kinda way when her friend came strutting in wearing a skintight wine colored satin dress, with a deep V neckline, spaghetti straps and a front slit. It was a jaw dropping number a woman wore when she didn't come to play.

Vannette looked down at her simple little black dress and felt she wasn't in Brianna's league tonight.

"Sorry I'm late but I got held up," Brianna said taking a seat.

"No worries. Let me pour you some champagne," Clayton said handing her a glass. "I want to introduce you to D-Boy when he finishes his conversation." He nodded his head in the direction D-Boy was sitting.

"Are you talking about D-Boy the rapper?"

"Yes. He's here with his manager who I'm considering doing some business with. I'm positive he would love to meet you."

Brianna gave Clayton an engaging gaze like she was down with meeting the popular rapper but she had zero interest. To Brianna dating a rapper was equivalent to dating a rich drug dealer. The only difference was one was on the stage and the other on the streets.

"Baby, I'll be right back. I need to use the restroom," Vannette said wanting to put on a little extra makeup, so she didn't feel so plain sitting next to Brianna.

Brianna was thrilled when Vannette left the table. It finally gave her some alone time with Clayton. She knew the opportunity might not present itself again, so she decided to strike.

"Are you ready to go meet D-Boy?"

"No. D-Boy isn't my type."

"Really? I thought women liked rappers," Clayton gave a sly smirk.

"Some do but I don't. I prefer a different type of man."

"What type of man is that?"

"A man like you." Brianna wanted to be blunt and direct. She had no time to waste.

Clayton gave her a look of approval. "I see you have more than just good taste in clothes."

"I'm glad you noticed."

"Isn't that the reason you wear a dress like that, to get noticed."

"As long as it worked."

"It did do that. D Boy hasn't stopped eyeing you. I would appreciate if you go over there and at least talk to him for a minute. Consider it a personal favor," Clayton stated.

"And what do I get in return for doing you this favor?"

"Tell me what you want and I believe we can make it happen. I'm always open to negotiations."

"I want you, so make that happen." Brianna got up and went over to speak to D-Boy and all Clayton could do was laugh.

"What's so funny?" Vannette asked when she returned from the restroom.

"Your friend. I like her."

"It seems D-Boy does too," Vannette remarked noticing the two seemed to be having an in-depth conversation.

"That's nothing," Clayton casually commented. "Vannette, I want you to do something for me."

"Sure, what it is?"

"Before I ask, remember I don't like the word no."

"You'll never hear me say that word to you," Vannette swore, sounding full of devotion.

"I can't believe I'm Mrs. Hernandez," Ashton beamed staring at the 10.16 carat, natural Columbian emerald, square cut ring on her wedding finger. The classic vivid green color sparkled perfectly against the melanin in her skin tone.

"I wish I could've given you a wedding that matched the beauty of the ring on your finger," Damacio told his new bride.

"Baby, you gave me the best wedding a girl could want. I had everything I needed, which is you." Ashton slid closer to Damacio on the bed. "You're my husband and I'm your wife. Nothing or no one can come between us, including my father."

Damacio kissed Ashton on her forehead. "My beautiful wife. I love saying my wife."

"I love you saying beautiful." Ashton and Damacio both laughed. "Why can't we stay in Vegas for at least the next six months. You can even open a club here. We have each other."

"I know but we can't escape reality forever," Damacio said stroking Ashton's hair. "We have to get back to Houston. I also want to speak to my father and try to end this feud he has with your father."

"I want to help with that too."

"No, Ashton. Let me deal with this. I don't want you caught up in the middle of this feud."

"I voluntarily got caught up when I told you I was ready for us to get married. How about this. I'll let you handle the heavy lifting when it comes to your father and mine but I do have to let my parents know I'm a married woman." Ashton flashed her ring. "I can request some unity now that the Hernandez and Collins are family," she smiled nuzzling her nose against his. "No more talking, we're in the honeymoon suite. It's back to making love."

Clayton was sprawled out comfortably on his king sized bed with Vannette lying naked beside him. When Brianna came out the bathroom wearing a satin bra and panty set that matched the wine colored dress she'd worn earlier, perfectly, regret instantly set in for Vannette.

"I don't think this is a good idea," Vannette spoke nervously.

"We agreed I don't like the word no."

"I'm not saying no."

"If you're not saying yes then you must mean no. Which one is it, Vannette?"

"It's yes," she said somberly like someone had died. That someone was Vannette's soul. She was willing to sell it, if it meant she had a real future with Clayton. But when Brianna crawled into bed, sharing an intense gaze with Clayton, Vannette knew that would never happen. The woman she'd looked up to as a mentor, when it came to playing men for money, had played the ultimate game on her. Brianna wanted Clayton for herself and she showed up to win.

Clayton leaned in to kiss Brianna but instead of putting her lips on his, she got right down to work and started kissing his dick. She took notes when Vannette mentioned how much Clayton loved getting his dick sucked. Brianna put all her deep throating skills to good use on her mark.

Vannette saw the unbelievable pleasure Brianna was bringing Clayton. She never remembered him looking at her that way with such lust in his eyes. It made Vannette cringe.

"Are you ready to feel inside this wet pussy?" Brianna glanced up and asked Clayton seductively as if Vannette wasn't even in the room. In mere seconds, she'd become a non-factor in what was supposed to be a ménage a trois.

What came next had Vannette ready to kill herself. Clayton ripped off Brianna's bra and panties with unrelenting passion and slid inside her raw. He'd always been an advocate for wearing condoms. Clayton kept a box in his drawer next to his bed and one downstairs in the living room in case he didn't have time to take the sex upstairs. Now here he was dicking down a woman he barely knew with no protection. Vannette couldn't stand watching this fuck fest unfold in front of her eyes any longer. She ran out the bedroom but it didn't matter because no one noticed.

Chapter Twenty-Five

New Beginnings

"Are you sure this is what you want to do? Your kids are grown. There is no reason you have to stay married to Allen," Gayle said to Karmen during one of their weekly chats by the pool.

"Trust me, I thought long and hard about it. It's not about our children. I know they would support whatever decision I made. My son Clayton would probably be happy if I left his father. He doesn't think he deserves me," Karmen sighed.

"He doesn't, but of course a son is protective of their mother and you have always been close to Clayton."

"Very close. Clayton really is a gentle soul although he does a good job of hiding it from most people," Karmen laughed thinking of her son. "But even he's accepted I've chosen to stay in my marriage."

"Can I ask why...why are you choosing to stay with a man who I know has broken your heart?"

"Yes, he's broken my heart but I still love him. I also believe he is done with Crystal and has learned his lesson."

"How can you be sure?"

"I'm not taking any chances. I still have Randall, the private investigator you recommended, on retainer. I know it's only been a couple weeks since Allen has begged for my forgiveness but so far so good. My husband has been on his best behavior."

"Allen is a very smart man. He knows what an incredible wife he has. Now that he realizes he could lose you, I'm sure he'll get his act together," Gayle said flatly.

"I hope you're right. I really don't want to squander anymore of my time worrying if my husband is being unfaithful. Especially now that my daughter is a married woman."

"Girl, I still can't believe little Ashton is married," Gayle shook her head. "She was always so free spirited even as a child. I didn't think no man could tame her. Hell, I didn't think she wanted to be tamed," Gayle joked.

"Forget free spirited, Ashton was just wild," Karmen giggled. "She was such a handful and the way Allen spoiled and gushed over her only made it worse."

"I bet he is devastated his baby girl is now married."

"You have no idea." Karmen reached for her wine choosing not to reveal the intricate details about her daughter's new husband to her best friend. Gayle had no clue about the other side of the family business and Karmen intended to keep it that way.

When Crystal heard the doorbell ring, she looked in the hallway mirror to check her hair and makeup. She unbuttoned her shirt to show some cleavage but then decided against it. "You don't wanna look like you're selling pussy. Keep it classy," Crystal said out loud before going to open the door. "Kasir, thanks so much for coming."

"I was reluctant but you said it was important so I came."

"It is. Please come in."

Crystal lead Kasir into the living room to sit down. Her new apartment wasn't extravagant like the high rise penthouse Allen had her stashed in but at least she could now have male visitors.

"Can I get you something to drink?" she offered.

"No. I'm good. I haven't heard from you in weeks. Why the phone call?"

"Kasir, the last time we saw each other, you said not to call you until my relationship with the married man was over."

"Who ended it?"

"It was mutual," Crystal lied. "There's no hard feelings between us," which was true, "but he wants to work on his marriage and I want to try and have a real relationship with you."

"Crystal, it isn't that simple. I don't know if I can trust a woman who would carry on an affair with a married man."

"That's understandable. I'm not asking you to jump into a fully fledged relationship with me. I'm asking for you to give me a chance to earn your trust, starting today."

"Okay."

"Okay...what?"

"I want to try and see where things go between us. But no more lies, Crystal."

"I promise. No more lies." Unfortunately for Crystal that was one promise she wouldn't be able to keep.

"Officer Bradley, thank you for meeting me on such short notice. Please have a seat." Allen closed his office door. "First, I want to thank you again for handling the situation at the nightclub for me. The Haitians were able to do what I needed, without anyone being arrested and that's all thanks to you."

"I take my job seriously, especially when it comes to you. You've always been very generous to the HPD and it hasn't gone unnoticed or unappreciated."

"I'm glad you said that because in the next couple of weeks, things might get a bit chaotic again and I'll need your support."

"Then you'll have it. Just give me the word and I'll have my men in place."

"Thank you and as always the appreciation is mutual," Allen said handing the police officer an envelope of cash on his way out the door.

Before Allen could sit back down, he could hear his assistant, who normally spoke in a soothing tone, speaking loudly to someone.

"Sir! You can't go in there! Sir!" Her voice became louder the closer she got. "Mr. Collins, I'm so sorry. He insisted on seeing you. Do you want me to call security?"

"Catherine, it's fine. I'll take it from here," Allen said closing his door. "Damacio, I would offer you a seat but since you won't be staying long you can stand."

"Allen, if you had answered my phone calls, I wouldn't have needed to show up at your place of work."

"Now you know how Kasir and I felt when we couldn't get in touch with you and your father. But there is one huge difference. I was looking for the product I'd spent millions of dollars on, you're simply being a nuisance."

"I didn't agree with how my father handled the situation and I told him so. But I want to make it right."

"How would you go about doing that, Damacio?"

"I want to give you the money we owe you with interest."

"I see. Did Alejo approve this?"

"No. It will come from my personal funds but I believe it shows I'm trying to make a good faith effort to resolve the issues between our families."

"What it shows me is you're trying to kiss my ass because you're married to my daughter. 'Cause you damn sure wasn't making these concessions before," Allen scoffed.

"Allen..."

"Don't Allen me!" he barked cutting Damacio off. You and your family rob me and now you've stolen my daughter and you think giving me back money you owe me, will make everything right. Get the fuck outta here! The only way you'll make this right is to leave Ashton alone."

"With all due respect sir, that will never happen. Ashton is my wife and it will stay that way," Damacio made clear.

"We'll see about that. You can get the hell outta my office. Now!"

"I can't stop staring at your ring," Vannette professed to Ashton, as the women enjoyed a milk and honey ultimate massage.

"I can't stop staring at it either. Damacio has such exquisite taste. He's even having a house built for us. If you could see the design layout, it's amazing," Ashton gushed.

"How does it feel being a married woman?"

"Unbelievable in the best possible way. Do you know I haven't popped any pills or done any type of drugs since the shooting at the club? I haven't felt the need. I'm already experiencing the ultimate high by simply being in love."

"I'm really happy for you, Ashton. Hopefully I'll find love one day too," Vannette said not sounding very optimistic.

"What's happening with the one guy you're seeing? I can't think of his name but you came to Damacio's club opening with him."

"You mean Jeff. He was someone I was seeing until Clayton came around."

"You're still hung up on Clayton," Ashton rolled her eyes. "I love my brother, I really do but he's such a selfish prick. He can't help himself."

"It doesn't matter, he's moved on."

"Moved on...like in a girlfriend? Clayton hasn't had a girlfriend since high school and it was only for a week, so he could have sex with her. After that, he dumped her."

"Hopefully he'll dump Brianna too," Vannette said before she burst out crying."

"Omigosh, Vannette are you okay!" Ashton didn't realize how upset her friend was and felt horrible. "Can you please excuse us for a moment please," she told both the masseuses.

After the women were alone, Vannette began crying even harder while Ashton did her best to console her.

"I agreed to do a threesome with Clayton and my

friend Brianna but it turned into a twosome which didn't include me," Vannette said between sniffles. "I only agreed to do it to make Clayton happy but it totally backfired."

"My brother is such an asshole," Ashton seethed. She hated seeing Vannette in so much pain.

"I don't blame Clayton, though."

"Why not? He's the one who asked you to do it."

"Brianna had her eyes set on Clayton and used me to make it happen. She basically admitted it when I confronted her a couple days after everything went down."

"What?!"

"Yes," Vannette nodded wiping away her tears. "She moved here from New York to be with her boyfriend. I didn't know this but they're having problems so Brianna decided she needed a new boyfriend. I made the mistake of telling her what a great catch Clayton is and I was hoping to be the one."

"Stop blaming yourself, Vannette. You got taken by two selfish, self-centered jerks. Brianna is clearly no friend and Clayton, well he's only friends with himself."

"But I love him."

"Vannette, you might think you love Clayton but you love what he represents."

"You mean because he's good looking, rich, smart, and can have any woman he wants. Of course, I love what he represents. I would be a fool not to."

"He also can be cruel and insensitive. I mean look what he did to you. Do you really want to build a life with a man like that?"

"Ashton, your life has always been a fairy tale and of course you've found your prince charming but that isn't most women's reality and it's certainly not mine," Vannette complained.

"I hear you but I think you deserve better than Clayton. It's doesn't matter what I believe though, it's what you believe. No matter what, I'm here for you, Vannette...always," Ashton said holding her friend as she continued to cry in her arms.

Chapter Twenty-Six

It's Over

"Man, that lil' motherfucker tried to tell me his dog ran off with his bag of my money and he don't know where he hid it," Darius chuckled. "I told that stupid nigga if he didn't bring me my fuckin' bread, I was gonna send his mama his body parts in a brand new refrigerator."

"Nigga, you been watching way too much of that show *Narcos*," Caesar laughed. "Speaking of *Narcos*, this Alejo. Let me answer this. Hello."

"Caesar, how are you?"

"I'm good. But you probably already knew this given how many times I've had to re-up."

"Yes, indeed. Our business arrangement has been very profitable. I anticipated it would be but that's not why I'm calling."

"Why are you calling, Alejo?"

"I need for you to do a favor for me. Can I count on you, Caesar?"

"Yes, you can."

"I knew it. We're going to have a very close relationship, Caesar. I'll be in touch soon to tell you exactly what I need."

"What did the old man want?" Darius asked when Caesar hung up.

"Not sure. Said he'll be in touch later on. Whatever it is, I'm sure it'll be interesting. I think he's..." Caesar stopped talking when he heard Brianna come in.

"Wifey's home," Darius joked when they heard Brianna coming downstairs.

"Man, I think it's time for me to have the conversation. I've been putting that shit off long enough," Caesar huffed.

"I need to go, anyway."

"You don't have to leave."

"Nigga, I wanna leave. I don't wanna be here when you tell Brianna you ready for her to bounce," Darius laughed. "Call me later," he said grabbing his car key.

"Hey, Darius," Brianna smiled as they passed each other on the stairs.

"Brianna." Darius replied with the one word and kept it moving.

"Darius seemed to be in a rush," Brianna said giving Caesar a kiss.

"He has some business to tend to. How was your day?"

"It was cool. Did a little shopping, got my nails done. You know the typical. I was thinking we could go out to dinner tonight. Maybe that restaurant we both love so much."

"We need to talk." Caesar sat down on one of the leather theater chairs and looked Brianna directly in the eyes. She already knew what Caesar was going to say before he said it. She was hoping if she stayed out of his way, she could prolong the inevitable. Her time was now officially up. Brianna wasn't completely assed out because for the last couple months she'd spent half the money Caesar gave her and stashed the other half. She wanted a full six months of security money, now Brianna had to figure out another way to score it.

"What is it, baby? What do you wanna talk about?" Brianna questioned as if clueless.

"I'm not gonna bullshit you, Brianna. We've been dealing long enough where I shouldn't have to."

"Of course. We've always had each other's back. I would do anything for you, Caesar," she said playing on his need to keep a woman around him that he could trust.

"I know, Brianna. You've proven I can sleep with both eyes closed around you. You cool people but it's not working on a romantic level anymore. It's time you go back home."

"What are you saying, Caesar? I don't understand." Brianna started putting on the waterworks, implementing the next part of her plan.

Caesar wasn't used to seeing Brianna cry or appear vulnerable. She was BK to the fullest and it was softening him up. "Yo, please don't cry."

"You said you cared about me, Caesar. When you asked me to come here, I thought that meant you wanted a future with me. At first, I missed New York but not anymore. I love Houston and consider it home. Now you want to send me back," Brianna sobbed.

"I hate to see you like this but I don't want to keep you around knowing the relationship ain't going nowhere. It's not fair to you."

"Oh, but it's fair to send me back to New York when there's nothing there for me? You know I'm not close to my family. Having you and Vannette here made me forget about all that."

"Brianna, what can I do to make this right?"

"You can start by not giving up on us. I can do better, Caesar...make you happy." Brianna was laying it on thick. She checked out of her relationship with Caesar weeks ago. Once he stopped wanting to have sex with her, not even a blowjob, she knew there was no way to save this sinking ship. Brianna was a hood chick but she wasn't a dummy. Caesar was much more inclined to throw her a bone if she pretended to be emotionally devastated by their breakup, instead not giving a fuck because she had her eyes set on another man.

"There's nothing you can do to make me happy, Brianna. I'm over it. But I do care about you and I wanna make this as right as I can."

"So, it's really over between us?" Brianna asked. She faked holding back more tears as if trying to be strong.

"Yeah it is. But I'm not gonna leave you out there, Brianna. I won't send you back to New York empty handed."

"I don't want to go back to New York. I want to stay here in Houston."

"I don't think that's a good idea."

"Why?"

"Because it might give you false hope. You staying in Houston might make you think there's a chance we'll get back together and that's not gonna happen."

"I'm not going to pretend that losing you is easy. It really fuckin' hurts. I love you, Caesar. I thought you were the one but I won't embarrass myself. If it's over, I have to accept that. I won't stalk you, text, and call you all day, every day. I won't call you at all if that's what you want. But please let me stay here in Houston. If you can help me out until I get on my feet. I won't bother you, Caesar. I promise."

"Fine. You can keep the car you've been using and I'll give you more than enough to rent you a crib for up to a year."

"Can you do one more thing for me?"

"What is it?"

"I appreciate the car and the money but I have to find a way to take care of myself, which requires a skill. I always wanted to attend school for hair and makeup. Eventually open my own salon. Would you please pay for me to attend school?"

"I respect anyone who wants to make a living and willing to put in the work to make that happen. So yes, Brianna, I will give you the money to attend school and I hope you become the most successful hair stylist in the city of Houston."

"Crystal, I never see you anymore. Now that you're with that Kasir dude you have no time for your girl. We hung out way more when you were seeing the married man," Remi spat.

"Well, that's because he had a wife. He wasn't free to actually date me and take me out all over town. I forgot how much I missed that until I started dating Kasir."

"I feel you but I miss my friend. Why don't we go to that new lounge tonight?"

"I have plans for tonight."

"Let me guess, with Kasir."

"No, it's one more thing I need to do, so I can free myself of the past and focus on my future with Kasir."

"Sounds serious."

"It is but once it's over, I can move on with my life. How about we go to the lounge tomorrow, my treat," Crystal beamed with excitement.

"Perfect! I'll call you tomorrow, chica!"

Once Crystal got off the phone with Remi, she went to take a shower to get ready. Tonight had to be perfect. There was no room for error so Crystal had to prepare accordingly.

Chapter Twenty- Seven

Out Of Options

"You get more gorgeous every day," said Damacio holding Ashton in his arms. "Once this house is done…"

"You mean this mansion," Ashton jumped in and said. "This place is humongous."

"Big enough to fill up with lots of beautiful babies."

"Instead of lots, let's start with two, my love."

"I can start with two. I'll convince you about having more while we're making love," Damacio said.

"I know you will. Our baby will do one thing for sure."

"That is?"

"Bring our family together. My parents would love a grandbaby."

"So, would mine. He's been wanting me to give him a grandson, forever."

"When are you going to let me meet Alejo or should I call him my father in law?"

"Soon, baby. He's going to adore you just like I do."

"You better. Now let's go. It was good seeing the progress being made on the house but I'm starving and we ain't got a kitchen here yet."

"We do need to go. I have a meeting in an hour."

"Does that mean you can't have lunch with your wife?"

"I'm sorry I can't, baby, but let's do dinner tonight at your favorite restaurant, and wear the backless white dress I love so much with no panties."

"How are you able to give me an orgasm with simply the sound of your voice."

"The same way you make my dick hard by just looking at me."

"We really are soulmates aren't we."

"Yes, we are." Damacio and Ashton stood in the circular driveway kissing like this would be the last time they'd ever hold each other again.

"Mrs. Collins, a package was just delivered to you," Bernice announced.

"I'm in my office. You can bring it in here, Bernice,"

Karmen yelled out, as she finished up placing an order online.

"Here you go," Bernice said placing the package on the desk. "Are you ready for me to bring you lunch?"

"As a matter of fact, I am. Who knew I would work up such an appetite doing some online shopping," Karmen giggled picking up the package Bernice brought her.

"I'll be back shortly," Bernice said leaving.

"That's strange, there's not a return address on here," Karmen commented reaching for the solid brass opener, after noticing an envelope inside. "A DVD." She hesitated for a second before sliding it into her laptop.

At first Karmen heard voices but no visual. It was a casual conversation but based on what they were discussing, it was very recent. Once the image came across her screen she saw Crystal undressing Allen before taking off her clothes and getting in bed with him. They appeared to be in a hotel room. So much for the business trip he told his wife he was on.

It was obvious to Karmen that Allen and Crystal were about to engage in sex and she had seen enough but her finger would not allow her to power off. She sat and watched as he had sex with another woman. The woman he swore was out of his life. Even the private investigator she hired said they were done. After two months of no activity, she told Randall he could stop surveillance. Now Karmen realized her husband was behaving like the snake he was. He slithered into hiding until he felt it was safe to come back out and engage in his trifling ways. This time Allen went too far. It's one thing to suspect your husband is cheating or even to know he has cheated, but to see it with your own eyes changes a woman forever. A part of your heart dies and nothing can bring it back to life.

Clayton arrived at the apartment he kept in downtown Houston. He used it primarily for his illegal business meetings but today he was using it to meet with someone who had become much more valuable.

"You said it was urgent. What can I do for you, Crystal?" Clayton asked pouring himself a drink.

"I did everything you wanted. I convinced Allen to meet me at the hotel, so we could have sex one more time and I even recorded it, just like you asked. You promised me if I delivered, I could get out of our arrangement. I've done my part, I need you to do yours."

"You did do your part. The video you provided served its purpose," Clayton stated, only imagining how angry his mother must've been when she received the DVD delivery. Clayton justified his cruel act by telling himself his father didn't deserve his mother and she needed to see him for the man he truly was.

"Good, then cut me loose."

"The pay is excellent, Crystal, so why are you so anxious to end our business arrangement."

"I'm just over this. I want to move on with my life."

"Move on with Kasir?" Clayton cracked.

"How do you know about Kasir?" Crystal fidgeted with her nails nervously.

"You really are dumb but I already knew this. That's how you got yourself in this predicament in the first place. You're an investment. I keep a close watch on all my investments. Kasir is my brother. You've been fucking father and son. I find it all extremely hilarious," Clayton mocked.

"I'm gonna be sick," Crystal said holding her stomach.

"Did you think you had a future with my brother? I mean does he even know your real name?" Clayton teased. "I hired you because you've mastered the skill of fucking and that doesn't require you being smart. Stick to what you know."

"You heartless sonofabitch. I'm going to tell Kasir what you've done. Maybe he won't forgive me but he damn sure won't forgive you. Exposing you is all the satisfaction I need," Crystal threatened.

"Listen to me carefully, Crystal. You're a whore. A whore who is being very well compensated for your services. You can continue to be a whore with benefits and work for me, or you can be somebody's whore in a federal prison. It's your choice."

"You told me you made those charges go away?"

"And I did for the time being. But just like I made them disappear I can miraculously make the charges reappear. Is your infatuation with my brother worth that to you? Do you think he'll come visit you in prison?"

"I just want my life back."

"It's yours. Continue on like you've been doing.

I have no problem with you seeing my brother. You fuckin' the hell outta him will probably take his edge off and help him relax. So, keep doing what you're doing," Clayton smiled.

He observed Crystal sitting pretty on the couch with her olive green off the shoulder sweater and matching skirt. Her hair was pulled up in an updo with a soft makeup look. She resembled a classy lady. "I take it you're meeting Kasir when you leave here?"

"I was meeting him for lunch but..."

"But nothing, Crystal. Go be with Kasir. Like I said, you can have your life back."

"So you say, but it's not the life I want," Crystal said grabbing her purse. "I really hate you, Clayton, and I pray you get everything you deserve."

"Maybe I will but it won't be from you. Now carry on. I'll be in touch when I require your services again."

Clayton dismissed Crystal and went back to business as usual. Knowing he more than likely ruined his parent's marriage made Clayton confident to make his next move.

Chapter Twenty-Eight

Nightmares

Allen's chauffer driven Maybach pulled up to his sprawling estate that rested on top of a bluff, embellished with multi-tiered gardens, fountains, terraces, and guard gated access. The breathtaking foyer and spectacular floating grand staircases were indicative of the powerful architectural detail and quality of the 18th-century style home. The unique residence had an elegant old-world exterior true to its classic design married to a sophisticated technologically enabled interior.

There were two reception salons, and an elegant

music room that was specifically designed for Karmen. All the rooms meshed peacefully into entertaining on all levels—informal gatherings, plated dinners, or standing cocktail receptions. Glass doors opened to the rear gallery porch and multi-level outdoor garden terraces. The far reaching beauty of the impressive grounds were only heightened by the incomparable view. The grandiose estate was the dream home Allen and Karmen had created together. That dream was now about to become a nightmare.

"Bernice, where is my lovely wife?" Allen asked putting down his suitcase.

"I'm not sure, Mr. Collins. She went out about an hour ago."

"Let me try calling her again," he said but still getting no answer. "Bernice, I'm going to head back out. Can you please take my suitcase and put away my things."

"Of course, Mr. Collins."

"If my wife comes home before I return, please tell her to give me a call."

"Will do, sir."

"Where to, Mr. Collins?" his driver asked once back in the car.

"Take me to Brennan's. I just got a text from Clayton saying he and Kasir were there. They want to discuss some business."

"Okay, sir. You can let them know we're on the way."

Karmen walked up front stairs in a teal drop neck sleeveless dress. She had a deep side parting, with her hair flung over her right shoulder. The dress stopped right below her knees, accentuating her perfectly sculpted calves from her years of being a professional dancer. With each step, she hesitated and questioned her decision up until the door opened and she saw his face.

"Karmen, I wasn't sure you were going to come."

"Me neither. I've changed my mind at least six times from the time I stepped out my car, until I knocked on your front door."

"You do know once you come in, everything changes. Are you ready for that?"

"I wouldn't be here if I wasn't."

"Then please come in."

Karmen stepped inside the house and Caesar closed the door behind them.

"Would you like for me to drop you off in the front, sir?," the driver asked as he pulled into the parking lot.

"That'll be fine," Allen said glancing out the back tinted window. "What is Crystal doing here?" he mumbled surprised to see her coming out of Brennan's.

"I'm sorry, I didn't hear you, sir."

"Nothing. You can stop here and let me out."

"Will do, sir. I'll be parked right here. Call me when you're ready and I'll pull up directly to the front."

Allen nodded his head as confirmation. While getting out the back of the car, he noticed Kasir come out and he was headed in Crystal's direction. He was shocked as his son took his mistress's hand. "Kasir!" he called out. At first his son kept walking, not hearing his father call his name due to the busy lunch crowd. Allen called out Kasir's name again but his time much louder. Kasir turned in his father's direction and waved his hand. While Kasir smiled at the sight of seeing his father, Crystal on the other hand wanted to run in the opposite direction.

"What in hell is Kasir doing with Crystal?" he said out loud ready to confront his son but before he could he saw the look of death in his son's eyes.

"Dad, get down!" Kasir belted with all his might, as a rapid-fire barrage erupted. It sounded like a machine gun due to the alarming rate the gunman was able to rain deadly rounds. The bloodshed was immediate and lethal.

Ashton was so high off love, she seemed to be walking on her tippy toes when she exited out the beauty salon headed towards her car. Her hair was freshly colored and blown out, flowing in the wind. Her rose gold, cat eye sunglasses might've disguised the sparkle in her eyes but just by the way Ashton's body moved, you knew the woman was loving life. Her head was so high up in the sky, that when the gray van pulled up behind her car and a man jumped out, she didn't have time to react. Before covering her head with a black pillowcase, he stuck a long thick needle in her neck, rendering her incapable of fighting back. The man tossed her limp body in the back of the van as the driver sped out of the busy parking lot, leaving behind Ashton's sunglasses, designer purse, car keys, and the brand new magnetic over rose gold Bentayga Mulliner that Damacio had gotten his wife as a wedding gift.

P.O. Box 912
Collierville, TN 38027

www.joydejaking.com
www.twitter.com/joydejaking

A KING PRODUCTION

ORDER FORM

Name:

Address:

City/State:

Zip:

QUANTITY	TITLES	PRICE	TOTAL
	Bitch	$15.00	
	Bitch Reloaded	$15.00	
	The Bitch Is Back	$15.00	
	Queen Bitch	$15.00	
	Last Bitch Standing	$15.00	
	Superstar	$15.00	
	Ride Wit' Me	$12.00	
	Ride Wit' Me Part 2	$15.00	
	Stackin' Paper	$15.00	
	Trife Life To Lavish	$15.00	
	Trife Life To Lavish II	$15.00	
	Stackin' Paper II	$15.00	
	Rich or Famous	$15.00	
	Rich or Famous Part 2	$15.00	
	Rich or Famous Part 3	$15.00	
	Bitch A New Beginning	$15.00	
	Mafia Princess Part 1	$15.00	
	Mafia Princess Part 2	$15.00	
	Mafia Princess Part 3	$15.00	
	Mafia Princess Part 4	$15.00	
	Mafia Princess Part 5	$15.00	
	Boss Bitch	$15.00	
	Baller Bitches Vol. 1	$15.00	
	Baller Bitches Vol. 2	$15.00	
	Baller Bitches Vol. 3	$15.00	
	Bad Bitch	$15.00	
	Still The Baddest Bitch	$15.00	
	Power	$15.00	
	Power Part 2	$15.00	
	Drake	$15.00	
	Drake Part 2	$15.00	
	Female Hustler	$15.00	
	Female Hustler Part 2	$15.00	
	Female Hustler Part 3	$15.00	
	Female Hustler Part 4	$15.00	
	Female Hustler Part 5	$15.00	
	Female Hustler Part 6	$15.00	
	Princess Fever "Birthday Bash"	$6.00	
	Nico Carter The Men Of The Bitch Series	$15.00	
	Bitch The Beginning Of The End	$15.00	
	Supreme...Men Of The Bitch Series	$15.00	
	Bitch The Final Chapter	$15.00	
	Stackin' Paper III	$15.00	
	Men Of The Bitch Series And The Women Who Love Them	$15.00	
	Coke Like The 80s	$15.00	
	Baller Bitches The Reunion Vol. 4	$15.00	
	Stackin' Paper IV	$15.00	
	The Legacy	$15.00	
	Lovin' Thy Enemy	$15.00	
	Stackin' Paper V	$15.00	
	The Legacy Part 2	$15.00	
	Assassins	$11.00	

Shipping/Handling (Via Priority Mail) $7.50 1-2 Books, $15.00 3-4 Books add $1.95 for ea. Additional book.
Total: $_____ FORMS OF ACCEPTED PAYMENTS: Certified or government issued checks and money Orders, all mail
in orders take 5-7 Business days to be delivered

CPSIA information can be obtained
at www.ICGtesting.com
Printed in the USA
LVHW111311300819
629518LV00001B/56/P

9 781942 217374